Other *Leisure* books by Johnny D. Boggs:

WALK PROUD, STAND TALL
CAMP FORD
EAST OF THE BORDER
DARK VOYAGE OF THE *MITTIE STEPHENS*
PURGATOIRE
THE BIG FIFTY
LONELY TRUMPET
ONCE THEY WORE GRAY
THE LONESOME CHISHOLM TRAIL

THE HART BRAND

Johnny D. Boggs

THE HART BRAND

LEISURE BOOKS NEW YORK CITY

Another one for Lisa and Jack.

A LEISURE BOOK®

May 2008

Published by special arrangement with Golden West Literary Agency.

Dorchester Publishing Co., Inc.
200 Madison Avenue
New York, NY 10016

ISBN 10: 0-8439-6029-9
ISBN 13: 978-0-8439-6029-7

The name "Leisure Books" and the stylized "L" with design are trademarks of Dorchester Publishing Co., Inc.

Printed in the United States of America.

10 9 8 7 6 5 4 3 2 1

Visit us on the web at www.dorchesterpub.com.

Prologue

In the spring of my fourteenth year, I rode for the Hart brand.

Today, that statement isn't so hard to imagine, but thirty-odd years ago the wind and sun hadn't turned my face to leather, my nose wasn't so misshapen, and I didn't stand so bowlegged. Fact is, in those days I could count the times I had been on the back of a horse on one hand. Shames me to admit it, but I grew up city-born, a "green pea" as you-all might say. All that would change in '96. Captain Hart saw to that.

The Panic of 1893 had been hard on my parents, struggling to stay off tick in the depressed economy of St. Louis, Missouri. We ran a mercantile, though Papa never had much of a head, or interest, for business. Keeping shelves stocked and the ledger balanced proved to be my mother's job, and with three other children—me being the oldest—taking her focus from our store while, seemed like, more and more folks bought their wares through mail-order outfits like Sears, Roebuck and Company, and Montgomery Ward, times had grown lean. So around Christmas of '95 my father declared it high time I earned my keep and became a man. St. Louis had a population of more than half a million, and growing, a lot of those folks hungry and looking for employment. That meant there was little work to be found for a fourteen-year-old—at least, nothing that paid enough to make it worthwhile and not offend my mother's staunch Methodist sensibilities. With Mama's reluctant help, Papa penciled a letter to his younger brother in New Mexico Territory, and, when the reply came, my parents scraped together what cash they could find and bought a railroad ticket to some place called Las Cruces. One of my uncle's riders would be waiting for me at the depot, he had written, and, if I proved a fit enough cowhand, I would earn thirty a month and found, almost all of that money to be wired back to my folks. If things didn't work out, I could seek employment elsewhere in the territory, and, well, Mama and Papa would have one less mouth to feed.

Looking back, I am certain my mother, who had been born in St. Louis and never even set foot outside of Missouri—not even crossing the river to Illinois, just to say she'd been there, which I had done at age six—would never have agreed to this apprenticeship had she known what lay in store. But we weren't soothsayers, and Mama, being business-minded, realized we desperately needed that money, reasoning that at least I'd be working for family, though she had not seen Frank Hart since her wedding. Still, Papa had a hard enough time getting her to relent, for his crooked legs, arthritic joints, scarred forehead, busted nose, and swollen knuckles did not exactly relieve her anxiety that cowboying was a safe profession, but he prevailed by wearing Mama down.

I wanted to go simply for the adventure, to see something other than hacks in a noisy city or bolts of calico and kegs of nails. I longed to feel something other than the miserable humidity, to escape the dreary skies, drab buildings, and that smell of stagnant water and Mississippi River mud. I wanted to touch the mountains and desert and smell the grass Papa always talked about.

Back in the olden times—and my father had been a relic long before I entered this world—Lucas and Frank Hart had cowboyed together in Texas and Kansas, driving herds of longhorns up the trails to such forgotten towns as Ellsworth, Grand Junction, and Caldwell. Frank Hart had saved his money and, through good fortune and an iron will, had carved an empire for himself in Lincoln County. My father, on the other hand, had never been the lucky Hart. One wreck too many on one rangy mustang too many left Papa too stoved up to cowboy, so he was pushing a broom in a stuffy mercantile when he met my mother.

He could tell stories, though, tales I cherished as a toddler but had outgrown as a teenager. By then, I figured Papa was full of fish stories and applejack, and found it just too hard to picture him, crippled as he was, as a man who had done any kind of work on the back of a horse. Yet his eyes beamed when my uncle decided to take a chance on me, and I can still see him so vividly, can smell the rye on his breath and Barber's Favorite shaving soap on his cheeks, as he limped to the depot with me on a bitterly cold January morning. He stuck a handful of peppermint candies, taken, I presumed, from the jar next to the cash register while Mama wasn't looking, in my coat pocket, along with a few wrinkled shinplasters and a couple of coins, perhaps all the cash money he had left.

Leaning his gnarled hickory cane against the wall, he pulled me close, not quite a hug, but as near to one as he could manage. "Write when you can. Your ma would appreciate that." He held out his callused hand, and we shook. "Frank can be a hard man, Caleb," he told me as tears welled in his own eyes, and mine, too. "But he's fair. You're a Hart, boy, and blood runs thick. Say your prayers, mind your manners, listen to your elders, and always remember this . . . you ride for the brand."

I had heard him use that phrase before, swapping lies and telling windies in front of the cracker barrel to any other old cowhand who would listen. Ride for the brand. I never knew what it really meant, though, but I would soon learn.

Captain Franklin J. Hart would teach me. In the rugged southeastern corner of New Mexico Territory, he'd teach me a bundle, more than 1,200 miles from the civilization I knew as home, and so would the friends I would make that year, cowboys, as they said, "to ride the river with"—men like Dickie Fergusson and Rex Steele and Kim Harrigan. And a couple of women, too. I'd have other teachers, folks I remember to this day, and many others I have long since forgotten.

Once winter gave way to spring, I would be riding for the Hart brand.

Eventually, though, I'd ride against the brand. Captain Hart saw to that, too.

Chapter One

Let's see. Where to start? Well, at the beginning, I guess, on the train ride from St. Louis to Las Cruces, and the time I met Kim Harrigan. He was the first cowboy I ever knew, not counting my father, of course, or any of those other broken-down old-timers who had rocked on stools around the stove in our mercantile and talked about days long gone. He was a working cowboy. I knew that from the worn but shiny saddle he threw with a grunt onto the seat across from me as the Atchison, Topeka & Santa Fé pulled out of Raton, New Mexico Territory.

As the cowhand took his seat, Mrs. Hudspeth—I never knew her first name—turned up her nose in distaste and pinched my arm, as had been her habit for the past 100 miles, to which the bruises on my forearm could attest. Since settling her bony frame next to mine at La Junta, Colorado, every time she wanted to say something snide about any of the passengers, she'd give me a painful pinch, lean over, and whisper into my ear, then straighten and suck on her dentures. I would have changed seats, but the railroad car was packed to the gills, and, Methodist upbringing and all, I didn't want to offend the old biddy, though I wondered if my arm would last to Albuquerque.

"The air has turned rancid, Master Caleb." Her cold eyes blazed at the cowhand sitting across from us. Her breath stank of Aromatic—a misnomer if ever there was—Cachou Lozenges, which she popped into her mouth with some frequency. Personally I preferred the smell of Papa's rye whiskey.

"Yes'm," the cowboy said, causing Mrs. Hudspeth to sit bolt upright as if she had heard a ghost. My eyes widened, too, amazed that anyone could hear the old woman's whisper over the din of the coughing locomotive and cacophony of voices inside the rocking car.

"It's them sodbusters," the cowboy continued, and he hooked a thumb toward a family of farmers a few seats up and over. "One of 'em just farted."

Well, I mean to tell you, I thought Mrs. Hudspeth would keel right over from cerebral apoplexy, and the stranger's comment caused my mouth to drop wide. Had I used such language, especially in front of a God-fearing elderly woman like Mrs. Hudspeth, Mama would have whipped my backside with a willow switch, and afterward Papa would have torn off the rest of my flesh with his razor strop. With a shaking hand, Mrs. Hudspeth somehow managed to open her bottle and toss another lozenge into her mouth. Then she got all haughty.

"I did not pay the Atchison, Topeka, and Santa Fé my hard-earned money to be exposed to such vulgarity," she snapped.

"No, ma'am," the stranger said. "And if them nesters keep fartin' like that, I'll be gettin' off at the next station with you."

I grimaced as her fingers dug into my flesh again, but this time she did not lean over to whisper a thing. She released her hold on my skin, stood up, and let out a—"Why, I never!"—before collecting her grip and storming down the aisle, out the door, and into the next car.

The cowboy gave me a wink, then stretched his long legs, propping his boots on the seat Mrs. Hudspeth had vacated, pulled his battered hat over his eyes, and started snoring within seconds.

His clothes looked new, nothing fancy but store-bought. Like I said, growing up in a mercantile, I knew about store-bought duds. The boots were older, their counters torn by years of rough use from spurs, though he wore no spurs now, and a plug of Even Change tobacco stuck out of his vest pocket. The hat was misshapen, stained from sweat and dirt, and his face resembled iron, forged by years in the elements, with a reddish-brown mustache, flaked with gray, that would have been the envy of many a tonsorial artist back home.

'Twas the saddle that gave him away.

A Wyoming stock rig, it barely fit in the seat next to him, and I knew it had to weigh more than thirty pounds with its steel fork, sixteen-inch tree, brass-bound stirrups, and wool-lined, thirty-inch skirts. How I knew so much about the stranger's saddle was because Papa had one in the mercantile for better than a year, priced at $60, which finally left the store—Mama had complained that it would never sell—about two weeks before I departed for New Mexico. This saddle looked scarred and used, but smelled of fresh saddle soap, and I remember Papa telling us kids as he vigorously worked a brush and rag against his proud possession: "You can tell a lot about a man from just looking at his saddle. A fellow may appear rougher than a cob, but if his saddle's clean, he's a good cowhand. If his saddle ain't, then he ain't fit to muck stalls."

Well, this saddle was clean, so he was a cowboy, and a good one, as far as my father would be concerned.

His name was Kim Harrigan, and he woke up south of Maxwell City.

I had been staring out the window, watching cows in the distance in this broken country of hogbacks, Spartan trees, and distant mountains. Suddenly a bolt of lightning struck the ground, raising a cloud of red dust, and the cattle bolted every which way. I jumped back in my seat, although the scene took place at least a quarter mile away, and the cowhand snickered.

"Some hobgoblin out there spook you?" he asked.

He pulled off his hat, revealing a bald pate, the paleness of the top of his head in stark contrast to the dark hair over his ears and that sunburned face. After fishing out his chewing tobacco and a folding knife, he carved off a sizeable wad, shoved the quid into his mouth, then held out the pouch of Even Change toward me.

"No, thanks," I said.

"Name's Harrigan," he announced. "Kim Harrigan."

I blinked.

"That's right. I got a girl's name." His voice had an edge now, but the dancing of his blue eyes let me know he held no anger toward me. "Nobody give me a choice about my handle when I was born."

"No, I'm sorry ... I mean ... I'm Caleb Hart. I was just ... it's not your name ... just. ..." I pointed outside. "Lightning struck the ground, scared some cows. I've never seen anything like it."

Nodding, he worked his tobacco silently, spit out a flake, and shoved his hat back on his head. "Some folks change their name faster than they change their unmentionables, but I figured, by grab, a name's the one thing nobody can take from you, and if my stupid pa wanted me to be named after a girl, well, I'll live with it. And fight anyone who insults me."

From the scars on his face and the crooked nose, I detected that he had defended his name many times over the years. "You ain't insultin' me, are you?"

"No, sir."

"Good." He moved the chaw of tobacco from one cheek to another, and changed the subject. "You'll see a lot of lightnin' in this country," he said. "Hit any cowboys?"

"No, sir. Didn't see any cowboys out there."

"That's good. Kill any cattle?"

"No. I don't think so. Just spooked them."

"That's even better. Did it fry any sheep-herders?"

"No. ..."

"That's a shame." He spit into the cuspidor, stretching his arms and legs. "You say your name's Hart?"

"Yes, sir. H-a-r-t."

To my surprise, and disappointment, he simply

nodded, pulled his hat down over his eyes, and fell back asleep, a huge bulge in his cheek. I thought we were beginning a conversation, that he would ask where I was bound, and then I could bombard him with questions about his saddle, working the range, lightning strikes, and any green-pea question that popped in my green-pea brain. Instead, I pulled out a copy of the New Mexican *Single-Taxer*, which someone had left behind, and read the newspaper again and again, while sucking on the last of the peppermint candies Papa had plundered.

Fact is, that turned out to be the bulk of our conversation as the train wound south, through Wagon Mound and Las Vegas, through Glorieta Pass, over to Lamy and down to Albuquerque, where Mrs. Hudspeth scowled at both Kim Harrigan and myself as she departed the train. Deep south we traveled, leaving the mountains and piñons behind and into a vast desert. Every so often, Harrigan would wake up, work his plug of tobacco, and ask for our location before drifting back to sleep. Belen . . . Socorro . . . Cutter, names that meant nothing to me, and, from the look on his face, held little interest to him. He slept so much, I wondered if he were sick.

Finally, as the train slowed to a crawl, the conductor walked down the aisle, checking his pocket watch as he announced: "Las Cruces!"

Kim Harrigan didn't budge as I stood and collected my carpetbag, hat, and overcoat, which, from the heat I already felt, I doubted I would ever need. Cautiously I stepped over his legs, wanting to tell him good bye, but daring not wake him. A man as tired as that, well, he needed his sleep. We hadn't talked much, but I thought I owed him a debt of gratitude. After all, he had saved my arms from Mrs. Hudspeth's incessant pinching. Yet the only movement I detected was the rising of his chest, which at least assured me that he hadn't died during the night. With a sigh, I followed a couple of drummers and stepped off the Atchison, Topeka & Santa Fé—finally—and walked around, lost, on the crowded depot.

Now what?

On my travels along the AT&SF line, I had seen some country. Kansas and Colorado had looked like a vast wintry expanse of plains, brutal in its nothingness, where the windows of the cars became frosted with thick coats of ice. Then we had climbed into the mountains, strained our way over Raton Pass and entered New Mexico, and I loved the scenery. Snow capped the mountains between Raton and Lamy, often covering the piñons. Lightning strikes . . . hundreds of antelope . . . frozen rivers and dry creekbeds. All romantic to an adventure-starved teen.

Nothing looked romantic here. The dust felt choking, and the mountains, looming in the eastern horizon, held neither snow nor piñons, just craggy rises spearing the sky, the setting sun staining those rocks with a crimson blaze. The warmth of the evening surprised me, and the spicy aroma of food pricked my nostrils. Conversations sprang up all around me, but I could understand none of the words, for most of the talk was in Spanish. In St. Louis, I had learned a bit of French here and there, which did me no good in this strange country.

Now what? I thought again, looking for some

familiar face. My uncle wrote that he would have a rider waiting for me, but how was I to know this man? My eyes sought out someone who resembled a cowboy, and, as the depot cleared, I noticed several who filled the bill, but I couldn't make my legs move.

"Fellow you're lookin' for is that *hombre* over yonder rollin' himself a smoke."

The voice I recognized instantly, and I quickly spun to see Kim Harrigan, looking wide awake, the bulge in his cheek gone, lugging that Wyoming rig over his shoulder. He jutted his chin out, and I followed that line to see a tall, thin man sitting on the tile floor, back braced against the adobe column, wetting a cigarette with one hand while striking a lucifer with the other.

"How?" I began.

"Said your name was Hart, didn't you?" Before I could reply, Harrigan continued: "Then I take it you're kin to Capt'n Hart, and that fellow has been ridin' with the capt'n as long as anyone can recall. Come on, Caleb. I'll introduce you."

The cigarette-smoking man saw us first and pulled himself up with a big grin, an infectious smile, I mean to tell you. Railthin he was, with sandy hair, mustache, and goatee, dancing eyes, and a sod-colored hat pulled practically down to his eyebrows. In his high-topped boots, he stood a good four inches taller than Kim Harrigan, and towered over me.

His hand shot out, and the smoke dangled from his lips as he said: "Kim Harrigan. Well, I'd bet my bottom dollar they'd never let you out of Wyoming."

"How you farin', Rex?"

"I'm finer than frog's hair. Reckon you seen the elephant?"

"Ain't seen much these past five years."

"Well, it's good to have you back, riding for the brand. Who's that nubbin of a shadow you got there?"

"This is Caleb Hart. Met him on the train, and I take it he's here to see the capt'n. Caleb, meet Rex Steele."

We shook hands, and, after taking a long pull on his smoke, he tilted his head southward. "Yes, sir, seems Caleb's daddy sent him down here to ride with us. Ain't that right, Caleb?" I couldn't get a word in, which would prove the case time and again whenever I got into a conversation with Rex Steele. "Caleb's pa is Frank's older brother. Reckon you heard Frank mention him a time or two."

"Seems like."

"Good timing, it is, Kim," Rex said, and he walked, pigeon-toed, toward a string of horses. "Wasn't sure you'd be here, but I'm glad you can ride along with us. Frank sent some of the boys over here to pick up his cousin. . . ."

"Nephew," Kim corrected.

"Well, pick up Caleb here, and then we could ride back to Lincoln with Colonel Fountain. The sorrel horse is yours, Caleb. Kim, we'll pick up a mount for you over at Lucero's." He swung into the saddle with ease, finished his cigarette, and tossed it into the dusty street.

Me? I was trying to figure out which horse was the sorrel.

The smile faded from Rex Steele's face as he looked down on Harrigan.

"You bring your rifle, Kim?"

I hadn't noticed the scabbard until then, not really, but Harrigan shifted the saddle until Rex and I saw the battered stock and case-hardened bolt of some kind of rifle Papa had never kept at the mercantile. A bandoleer filled with long, brass cartridges was wrapped around the bedroll tied behind the cantle. I hadn't noticed that, either.

Rex Steele nodded solemnly. "That's a good thing, Kim. Things been getting a mite dangersome."

Chapter Two

When we left the depot, I figured we would make a beeline for either this Colonel Fountain's place or the livery stable, but Rex mentioned the need to "irrigate" and moments later I found myself entering a smoke-filled *cantina* for the first time. Almost immediately a grinning Mexican bartender slammed two shot glasses in front of Rex and Kim, filling them with a clear liquid that had my eyes watering even from a distance. The bartender did not notice me.

"*Salud.*" Rex hefted his glass, but Kim, after dropping his Wyoming rig beside him, just stared at his glass on the dusty bar.

"It's on me, pard," Rex said.

"Spent my last coin on the ticket down here." Kim spoke in a hushed whisper. "Can't buy you one back."

"You're grubstaked, pard," said Rex, lowering his glass slightly. "You can pay me back, with interest, because I know Frank'll be paying you top wages, old hand. Now drink up."

Slowly Kim pushed the whiskey back toward the barkeep, whose smile had dimmed. "Well, in that case," Kim said, "seein' how it's been five years since I had a taste of liquor, I reckon I'll pass on this scamper juice." He pointed at a fancy bottle on the backbar just behind the bartender's shoulder. "Is that really Glenlevit or is it just forty-rod poured in a Scotch bottle?"

The bartender leaned forward, pressing his elbows on the bar while tugging on an ear-lobe. "You and *Señor* Rex, you are *amigos*, no?"

"We've rode a lot of country together," Kim said.

"Then, *amigo* . . . "—he pointed at the shot glass—"be kind to your soul. *Por favor*, drink this." Thumbing toward the bottle of Scotch, he made a face, shook his head, and added something in rapid Spanish that left both Rex and Kim laughing.

"An honest barkeep," Kim said when he had stopped cackling so loud, and, wiping the tears from his eyes, he picked up the glass and downed its contents in a gulp.

"What's it been, Kim, five years?" Rex motioned for a refill.

"Eight and a half."

Rex whistled, and sipped his drink this time. "Well, the country's changed. Times have changed."

"Uhn-huh. Quieter, seems like."

"Not hardly." Rex grinned. "Reckon that's why Frank asked you to come back home. Don't let tonight fool you. Las Cruces is still about to bust a boiler, especially when court's in session. And this whole country ain't nowhere near tame."

"Town's growed some."

"Sure has, Kim. Everything's growed. Even Frank. He has slapped his brand on pretty much everything from the Río Hondo all the way up to just south of Puerto de Luna. What he ain't branded, well, most folks, even the sheepherders, they know it's his country. Except some Texians. Them that are right handy with a wide loop and a running iron. You know that type."

"I'm familiar," Kim said. "Grew up in Texas myself."

Part of me wanted to taste my first whiskey, or whatever it was they were drinking, no matter how awful it smelled. Mostly, however, I wanted to be noticed, at least offered something to drink, even water if not a sarsaparilla or a ginger ale. Yet the two cowboys, intent on catching up and remembering old times, had forgotten all about me. I blamed it on the whiskey, much as my mother would have done.

"Capt'n Hart hails from Texas, too, if I remember right," Kim added. "Capt'n always was an ambitious sort. Lincoln County seems to bring that out in men."

"Yeah, but, unlike most of 'em, Frank has always rode with the law. Problem we have these days is with men like Oliver Lee. Had Lee settled here before you rode off to Wyoming?"

Kim finished his whiskey, but, when Rex motioned again for another refill, Kim shook his head at the bartender, who stood ready and willing to satisfy his customers.

"I seem to recollect Lee came in around 'Eighty-Four," Kim said. "Came from Texas, too. Had a little spread in the Tularosa Basin."

"Well, he has grown, too. Aims to be the biggest toad in the puddle." Rex cleared his throat when the bartender corked the bottle, grinned when the big man turned around, and mouthed—"One more time."—before pulling out the makings for another cigarette.

I began growing more restless, hungry, thirsty, and mighty irritated at being ignored. All this catching up could wait, I figured. At first I had been curious to enter my first saloon, but the smoke stung my eyes, and the whole place stank of stale beer and other odors I cared not to identify. One woman sat on a table in the corner, talking to a couple of bearded men in greasy buckskins, and she commanded my attention just briefly with her colorful outfit that revealed an obscene amount of thigh, but, when she looked over at me and grinned just for a second, I lost all interest. Her teeth were black, or so they appeared to me through the putrefying smoke, and I had never seen anybody wearing so much rouge. Slapped on like coats of paint, I mean to tell you. She laughed, too, when I quickly looked away, figuring, I warrant, that she had made me blush, but shyness hadn't been the reason. I found her repugnant. Didn't like her laugh, either. The men in buckskins, on the other hand, didn't mind at all.

"He's murdered quite a few men, including Walter Good and Frenchy Rochas, though nobody can prove it," Rex was saying, and I guessed he was still talking about this Lee fellow. "Cut down some others and claimed self-defense, and he's got himself some pettifogging lawyer just as bad as some of them gunmen riding for him. But what strikes us as curious . . . us meaning Frank and the colonel and me and just about any other honest rancher in this part of the territory . . . is how Lee's herd keeps getting bigger."

"While everybody else's herds keep gettin' smaller?" Kim said.

"Yep. Reckon you saw that up in Wyoming."

Kim didn't answer. His face turned hard, seemed to me, and he pushed off the brass foot rail, grabbed his saddle, and headed for the door, calling out to us that it was time to go pay Colonel Fountain a visit. Rex slammed down his whiskey and strode across the floor, with me trying desperately to keep up.

After Kim picked out a horse, a fine-looking bay gelding, at Lucero's livery, we rode to Water Street. When Kim said he thought the colonel lived in Mesilla, Rex informed him that the Fountains had moved to a bigger place, to be closer to the action since Las Cruces had the railroad and the courthouse.

"Think I recollect that now," Kim said, and knifed another cut of tobacco into his mouth.

I didn't like Las Cruces. It was ugly, raw, laid out in some haphazard fashion, streets lined with flimsy, weather-worn saloons. The streets weren't paved, but caked with a fine, thick dust, cluttered with three-armed poles strung with twenty-four electric lines, the only modern convenience I found, although in the corner of my eye I kept noticing Rex and Kim cast long stares at the bawdy houses, which, I guess, cowhands would consider a convenience.

Rex called Las Cruces a town that would rival St. Louis, but, now that the train had departed, I found little to be happening that evening other than a few dogs barking and a rooster, obviously out of sorts, crowing as if it were morning. By jacks, I doubted if Rex Steele had ever seen St. Louis.

Something had to be going on, however, at the large house on Water Street where we tethered our horses on a picket fence. Candles and lamps burned in every window, and at least a half dozen horses were hobbled or tethered to a hitching rail inside the thick adobe fence surrounding the home. Home? It looked more like a fort, with thick stone and adobe walls. It was dark by now, but a street lamp provided enough flaring light from its candle—*No gas lamps in this rival of Saint Louis*, I thought with a touch of sarcasm, still the big-city kid.

That's when I noticed the brand on my sorrel gelding. I traced its outline with my fingers, and suddenly forgot all about my hunger, thirst, watering eyes, and unkind sentiments toward Las Cruces.

A simple heart outline had been burned black in the gelding's red hair, and my mind raced back to our mercantile, hearing my father talk about riding for the brand, honor, things like that, and I suddenly felt like a man, or how I thought a man should feel.

"What do you think?"

Turning, I spotted Kim Harrigan grinning at me.

"It's smaller than some brands I've seen," I answered, and Kim broke out laughing.

Kim struck me as a moody sort, troubled maybe by something that had happened up in Wyoming, though that could have been attributed to nothing more than a fourteen-year-old boy's starved imagination. He could laugh with the best of them, almost as jovial as Rex Steele, but mention the wrong word or subject, and his brow would crease and the light would leave his eyes. I made myself a note to watch what I said around him. Right then, however, he acted like the joking, fun-loving Kim Harrigan who had upset Mrs. Hudspeth so, and not the taciturn fellow I had chased after out of the *cantina* forty minutes earlier.

"That's fittin'," he said. "Capt'n ain't got much of a heart no-how. Let's go see Col'nel Fountain."

As I said, the home danced with activity, and I thought perhaps a party was being held, but two somber men greeted us at the door. Both of them carried large-bore Marlin rifles.

They must have recognized Kim or Rex, because neither guard made an effort to block our path, and paid scant attention to me. Inside, Kim removed his hat; Rex left his on. I quickly scanned the house, but the numbers looked about even, half of the men wearing hats, the other half hatless. I followed Kim Harrigan's example. After all, he was my friend, and, besides, if the story ever got back to my mother, a willow switch would be awaiting me in Missouri.

"Mister Steele?"

The voice had to be described as commanding, but, I don't know, I guess hearing colonel-this and colonel-that for the past few hours, I had expected to meet a strapping figure like Buffalo Bill or George Custer, though I had only seen those two men in photographs and paintings. Albert Jennings Fountain didn't even wear a uniform, but a well-made dress suit of fine wool and a pretty silk cravat.

"Colonel Fountain." Rex shook the man's hand. "Captain Hart sent us along." Up till then, Rex had always called my uncle by his Christian name, but now he used the rank, though, recalling my father's stories, I didn't think Frank Hart had ever served in the military. "This here is Kim Harrigan. Used to ride for the captain but has been up Wyoming the past eight years. And this is. . . ." Shaking his head, he shot me a woeful stare. "I'm sorry, son. I disremember your name."

He had no problems earlier, but that had been three whiskies ago.

"Caleb." I decided to do my own talking. "Caleb Hart. Frank . . . er . . . Captain Hart's my uncle, sir." I held out my hand.

Not a big man, Colonel Fountain stood maybe just a shade shorter than Kim Harrigan, though ramrod straight instead of Kim's relaxed slouch and bowed legs. While the colonel spoke in a powerful voice, thus giving me the notion that he had at least once been in the Army, his face looked weary, a furrowed brow accenting the palest eyes I had ever seen, and one couldn't help but notice the wicked scar along his left temple. His hair was thinning, but his graying mustache remained long and thick. I figured him to be about sixty-five years old. Turned out, he was only fifty-eight. His grip, though, nigh about crushed my hand.

"A pleasure, Master Hart," he said, and looked back up at Rex.

"Captain Hart wanted some of us boys along to ride with you to Lincoln," Rex said.

After glancing at me, Colonel Fountain gave Rex a quizzical stare. "Boys?" he said jokingly.

"Well, Caleb, here. He come to town from Missouri on the train," Rex explained. "His daddy sent him out to work for the captain. We just picked him up at the depot this evening. Anyway, with court in session in Lincoln, things might get a bit ticklish, sir. But you know that already. Them two *hombres* at the door, I know them both, and they are full of cussedness."

"They are here at the direction of the Southeastern New Mexico Stock Growers' Association," the colonel said, "not mine. I do not know if they ease Mariana's fears, or add to her heartache."

His accent I couldn't place, not foreign or anything, but nothing that I had ever heard in St. Louis, and certainly educations away from the laconic drawls of both Kim Harrigan and Rex Steele.

"Be that as it may," Colonel Fountain said, "when do you desire that we take our leave?"

"First light."

"Very well."

"You taking anyone with you, Colonel? Them two boys at the door, for instance."

"No," he answered adamantly. "I didn't want them here in the first place, but bowed to the association and my wife."

"That's all right." Rex jerked a thumb toward Kim. "Kim here, he's handy with a rifle, ain't that right, pard?"

Kim grunted, the only sound he had made since walking inside. Like I said, Kim's humor could be shut off like an electric light, which I hadn't seen since Missouri.

"Take Henry with you, Albert!" I turned toward

the new voice, finding a delicate creature with hair the color of a crow's wing, a shiny silver crucifix dangling from her neck on a white blouse. I could not even fathom a guess as to her age, but she looked, as my father would have said, "as pretty as a basket of chips." Turned out, I'd later learn, that she was around forty-eight years old, but she had to be the prettiest woman that old—which isn't so old to me now—I had ever seen. She spoke in a Mexican accent as strong as the bartender's, and she sure made an impression. Rex Steele even swept off his hat.

"This is men's talk, Mariana," the colonel spoke in sharp rebuke, but the woman did not retreat.

"You are my husband," she said, then sang out a few more words in Spanish. "Men have threatened your life. You will not take those *asesinos* with you, to protect yourself. . . ."

"Perhaps I protect you and our children by leaving them here," he said.

"*Por Dios,*" she said, her voice now pleading. "Take Henry."

"You would have me shield myself using my own son, woman?" Now I knew that Colonel Fountain had definitely served in the military, for his tone left me trembling.

"They will not harm you," she said, tears streaming down her face, "if Henry is with you. Even they would not harm a little boy."

"And I will not hide behind one. Go to your room, Mariana. I will hear no more of this foolish talk."

He dismissed her, and just as quickly dismissed us with a cold, powerful stare. Rex donned his hat and told the colonel that we'd see him in the morn. He tipped his hat while Kim and I mumbled some "good evenin'" or "pleasure to meet you" barely audible to Mrs. Fountain, who had not obeyed her husband's instructions and just stood there, her black eyes matching, perhaps besting, the colonel's glare. We made our way through the house, off the porch, down the flagstone walkway, and through the creaking gate. No one spoke until we were trotting toward Mesilla, where we would camp the night in a wagon yard.

"Fountain used to not be so touchy," Kim Harrigan said. "I recollect him bein' downright witty."

"That's changed, too," Rex said. "But the colonel, boy-howdy, he sure put his wife in her place, didn't he, Kim?"

"Uhn-huh," Kim answered, but, to me, he sounded mighty skeptical.

Chapter Three

Breakfast that morning was coffee as potent, I assumed, as the forty-rod whiskey my new mentors had been drinking in the *cantina* the previous night. I mean to say that this coffee could float a horseshoe, perhaps a farrier's whole supply, but Kim Harrigan pulled me aside and taught me how to drink cowboy brew while Rex, feeling charitable, saw to our horses.

We had met up the night before with some other Hart riders who had camped at the wagon yard in Mesilla, just a couple of miles from Las Cruces. Rex had made the introductions, though I've long since forgotten most of their names. That morning, they tended their horses, all branded with that heart outline, some cleaning hoofs with picks, others rubbing them down, a few joking with Rex while rolling smokes.

"Rex Steele," Kim was telling me, "can teach you everything you need to know about horses. 'Bout the best I ever knowed. But his coffee'll kill you if you ain't built up a tolerance for it." He took my mug and dropped a handful of sugar cubes into it. "Wish we had an air-tight of milk. That helps take the sting out of this, but you'll have to grow up faster, I reckon. Anyhow, that's how I learned to drink his stuff. First I added milk and a passable amount of sugar. Weaned myself off the sugar first, then, once we was out on the range, didn't have no milk, like now, so I drunk it straight. Pretty soon, I had grown used to it, when a month later back at the bunkhouse, the cook . . . Capt'n's got himself a new cook since I been gone, right good, I hear . . . handed me some milk whilst I was fixin' me a cup, and, without thinkin', I added some. Took a drink, and 'bout spit it out. Without meanin' to, I had weaned myself of milk, and was drinkin' it straight. Now, most cooks boils his coffee with the sugar in it. That's how most of the boys like it, but Rex. . . ."

Rex had returned, smiling as usual, and sang out: "I take my coffee black, my smokes hand-rolled, my whiskey neat, my horses on the bronc'y side, and my women . . ."—the grin widened—"just as raw."

Fourteen years old, thoughts wicked, I tried to match Rex's smile. Some of the other cowhands laughed.

I found the coffee, after Kim's doctoring, passable, and Rex kicked out the fire. We mounted up and rode out of Mesilla, which had come to life with the morning sun. It had a population of at least a couple thousand, just a tad more than Las Cruces, and folks were wandering all over the little plaza as we rode through town. Mesilla I liked, found it charming, a quaint little village of adobe walls and cottonwood trees. Rex said it had once been the king city of Doña Ana County, but Las Cruces, having the railroad, was taking over.

We trotted the two miles back to Las Cruces and the Fountain home. The rugged Organ Mountains rose in the distance, and frost covered much of the ground. In daylight, without so many horses tethered and hobbled out front, the Fountain fortress looked less boisterous, modest even compared to mansions I had seen back home, albeit certainly more impressive than the weather-worn adobe shacks and *jacals* we had passed. Compared to the previous night, the place looked almost deserted. The two guards with the heavy rifles remained on the portal, although they had leaned their Marlins against the wall and sat on a bench, sipping coffee.

Talking to one of his older sons, Colonel Fountain stood by his Brewster Springs Corning buggy, one white and one gray horse in the harness. He held a large dispatch case in his left hand, and, when another son tossed a cowhide in the back of the wagon, the old man snapped: "Careful with that, Tom!"

In the buggy, bundled up in a heavy coat, sat the colonel's youngest son, nine-year-old Henry. Mrs. Fountain had won that fight, after all.

"If I was you," Rex whispered, "I wouldn't mention one word about that kid."

Kim snorted and spit out a mouthful of tobacco juice. "My mama raised me better than to go about makin' fun of a fellow like Col'nel Fountain."

"Ain't what I mean, pard," Rex said. "I mean saying one word to me about me telling you last night that the colonel had put his missus in her place."

"Rex," said Kim, in the brightest humor I had found him in yet. "You implyin' I'd make fun of you?"

We reined up, waiting to see if Colonel Fountain would invite us to step down. He didn't, dismissing his sons and climbing into the buggy with a grunt. A Winchester rifle rested in the driver's box between the colonel and Henry. "Are you gentlemen ready?" the colonel asked.

"Yes, sir," Rex answered for everyone.

"Have you had your breakfast?"

"Yes, sir."

My stomach growled in disappointment. I wondered if I'd ever get something to eat in New Mexico.

"Good. Then let's be on our way."

Inhospitable. That's how I first considered the country, a stark, dreary, dangerous desert. And it's how I'd describe most of the men we met along the road—although calling it even a trail would require some imagination. I thought up a joke—"Even the plants out here are armed. Why should the men be any different?"—and tested it one night on Kim and Rex, but they just nodded with barely perceptible smiles. Well, I had found it funny at the time.

Perhaps I grew inhospitable, too. I think about that every now and then, remembering young Henry Fountain. He was sickly, and quiet, but he had been born late in his parents' lives, and likely found himself to be a loner, a stranger among his many, many brothers and sisters. One of the Hart riders suggested that Henry and I could play together, keep each other company, being kids and all, but I bristled at such a notion. Fourteen-year-olds did not play with nine-year-olds. Besides, I had come West to be a man, not to play boyish games, especially with a kid so shy he scarcely left his father's shadow and mumbled when he talked. Maybe he's scared for his life, and I wondered if he knew of the threats against Colonel Fountain, wondered if his parents had told him why he was joining his father on this trip.

So Henry Fountain remained a stranger to me, and I a stranger to him, and I've always regretted that. If I close my eyes, I can picture him, squatting at the campfire, eyes refusing to rise above the licking flames, seldom more than a foot from his father. If he said more than two dozen words on the 100-mile journey to Lincoln, I'd be surprised.

The colonel, now, he was a stranger, too, though I sure wouldn't call him shy. I tried to learn as much about him as I could during that three-day trip, for he seemed to be a major figure in this country, possibly bigger than Captain Frank Hart. I reckon Colonel Albert Jennings Fountain remains something of a stranger to us all.

Some of the boys said they had heard he had been educated at Columbia College in New York, but others called that rumor bogus. He had first come to New Mexico Territory during the War Between the States, ridden out with the California Column, proudly wearing the blue. After the war, he had worked for a while in El Paso—back then they called it Franklin—and I'd later hear the colonel say as much himself. In Texas, he had served in the Legislature but had left the state after some sort of scandal, and a shooting that had given him the scar along his temple. How much of that is true, I can't say.

In New Mexico Territory, he settled in Mesilla

before moving his ever-growing family to Las Cruces, and made a name for himself practicing law and running a newspaper, which had folded some years back. Back in the early '80s, he had served in some militia outfit called the Mesilla Scouts, and I learned that's when he had first met up with my uncle. The scouts had helped conquer the Apaches, but, from bits and pieces of conversation I caught during our travels, Colonel Fountain held many Apaches in high regard. He had even interviewed the great warrior Victorio, killed back in 1880, and, well, I had heard stories about the great Apache warrior and I hadn't been born until after he had been killed by Mexican troops.

Mescalero Apaches were one thing, but Colonel Fountain, he didn't hold Texians in high regard, not most of them anyhow. With the Indian troubles over, the Mesilla Scouts had waged war against Texas troublemakers in the mountain towns of the territory. He'd won that war, too, mostly, and come out a hero, got promoted to colonel, and went back to practicing law. A few years ago, rustling had started up again, getting heavier and heavier, so concerned ranchers, including Captain Hart, had formed the Southeastern New Mexico Stock Growers' Association in March of '94. They hired Colonel Fountain as the lawyer. Now he was on his way to Lincoln, bound and determined to persuade a grand jury to hand down a bunch of indictments.

"Colonel," Rex said on our last night on the trail, "if I ain't intruding, how strong is your case against them skipjacks?"

His smile caught me off guard, for his mouth

had appeared to be in a permanent frown, and he placed his coffee cup at his side and stretched out his legs until his boots rested inches from the hot coals of our fire.

"Stronger than the prosecution's case against Billy Bonney," he said.

Someone snapped his finger. "That's right," one of our riders said. "You defended the Kid."

Another man chuckled and said: "Bet the reason they convicted Billy the Kid, Colonel, was because you knew him to be a rustler. Your. . . ."

Boy-howdy, that oaf picked the wrong thing to say, because the colonel went stiff as a board, and his words left me cold. "I defended Bonney, or whatever his name really was, with all my vigor, mister. The same as I prosecuted John Kinney, and with the same vigor as I will prosecute Oliver Lee and all his comrades bent on evil intent."

The man—Grover, I think was the name— mumbled a sincere apology, yet I suspect the colonel's mood would have remained frigid had I not spoken up.

"Who was Billy the Kid?" I asked.

Tobacco juice sizzled in the fire, and I knew Kim Harrigan had just spit. Every eye around that campfire locked on me, and I felt dumber than Grover.

"You a-joshin' us, boy?" one rider asked.

Meekly my head shook.

Yes, that's how big a green pea I was, but you need to understand. Folks knew William H. Bonney mighty well in New Mexico Territory, but he hadn't made much of a name for himself in the States at that time. Sure, when he broke out of the Lincoln County Courthouse and killed those two deputies, and a few months later, after Pat Garrett shot him dead, the newspapers back East ran a bunch of stories, and Charlie Siringo wrote about the Kid in his book about being a cowboy, but all that was before I was born, you see, and folks had forgotten all about him, at least in Missouri, by 1896. 'Course, that Mr. Burns fellow, he changed all that two, three years back when he got his book published, which strikes me today as pretty sad. Folks all over these United States know who Billy the Kid was, thanks to Mr. Burns, but you can scarcely find anyone outside of New Mexico who ever heard of Albert Fountain or Frank Hart.

The point I'm trying to make here is that William H. Bonney left a mighty big trail in southern New Mexico, but I didn't know that when I was a yonker.

"The Kid was a cut-throat," Colonel Fountain said, "but a charming one. He rustled cattle, and killed men in the Lincoln County War, and didn't stop killing. Judge Bristol appointed me to defend the Kid in 'Eighty-One for the murder of William Brady, sheriff of Lincoln County. I lost, and Billy was sentenced to hang."

"He broke out, and Pat Garrett shot him dead at Pete Maxwell's place in Fort Sumner," Rex interrupted, champing at the bit to add his insights on those days. Before Rex could launch into some big windy, however, I asked another question.

"And John Kinney?"

"A far more brutal man," the colonel said, warming up again. "I had the honor to both capture him and see him tried in 'Eighty-Three, and that was both an honor and a pleasure. We convicted him, despite his threats, and he was

sentenced to five years at Leavenworth. Alas, he
served only three, but he has dared not show his
face in this country since his release."

"And what of Oliver Lee?"

"The worst of the lot," Colonel Fountain said,
"but powerful, and he has a fine attorney, though
a man I find contemptuous, downright ruthless,
in Albert Bacon Fall."

"But can you convict him?" Rex asked, bringing us back to our original point.

The colonel smiled again, and pulled his son
closer, buttoning the top button of his coat. "Here,
Henry," he said warmly, "it is turning colder." He
wasn't kidding, either. In a matter of a couple of
days, we had climbed out of the bitter desert and
into pine-rich hills. This country reminded me
slightly of what I had seen in the northern part of
the territory, and the wind reminded me that it
remained January. Each day grew grayer, each
night colder.

Colonel Fountain turned back to face us. "I had
just hung out my shingle, a proud new member of
the Texas bar," he said, his voice warming as he re-
flected on his youth. "The county solicitor said he
had been impressed with one of my earlier cases,
only my second or third one, and asked if I would
help him prosecute a young man, a vile man, one
much like a John Kinney or an Oliver Lee. In some
senseless brawl in a dismal saloon, he had shot
down another young man, an unarmed man,
which the town marshal had witnessed. The marshal promptly arrested the defendant. By all rights,
this case was as simple as they came, and I wondered why the solicitor desired my help, but it was
my first big trial, a murder case, and I was eager.

"My excitement grew even more when the solicitor asked if I would handle the interrogation of the marshal." Colonel Fountain shook his head. "He was our lone witness, the only one we needed, and I jumped at this chance. I asked the marshal to describe the events he saw on the night of the shooting, and he did, with precise detail. I introduced the murder weapon, and he said, yes, that was the gun used in the killing. I asked him if he arrested the killer, and he said he had. I asked him to name that man, and he named the defendant. Smugly I looked over my shoulder. The defense attorney sat at the table, a finger picking at his ear, and I looked at the solicitor, who smiled and nodded at my legal prowess. I passed the witness, and the attorney said, to my surprise . . . 'No questions.' So, said I . . . 'Your Honor, the state rests.' I strutted back to our bench, proud as a peacock.

"Then, slowly, the defense attorney rose. 'Your Honor,' he said in a voice thick as hominy, 'did I hear correctly? Does the state rest?'

" 'Mister Fountain?' the judge asked, and I rose. 'Yes, sir, the state rests.' I had been so sure of myself, but, seeing that smirk on my opponent's face, I began to worry. The solicitor said nothing, did not even glance my way.

" 'Well, Your Honor,' the attorney said, 'I reckon the defense will rest, too, as soon as I make my motion here to have this case tossed out.'

"I jumped out of my seat, shouting, angry now . . . 'On what grounds?'

" 'The state left out one wee bit of evidence. Allmighty crucial evidence, though.' "

"Enraged, I was. The marshal, a man of impeccable character, had witnessed the shooting, had arrested the culprit, had identified both the weapon, a Colt revolver, and the defendant. The judge instructed us to approach the bench, and, when we did, I began my argument, reciting my case, but the lawyer . . . or should I say, shyster . . . stood like some cock-of-the-walk. When the judge turned to him, he shook his head and gave me a look of pity, or mockery.

" 'The state has rested,' he said. 'The state did not identify my client.'

" 'By thunder, the marshal most certainly did!' I yelled.

" 'By name only.'

" 'If you are trying to argue that Bob Smith isn't his name . . . ,' I began.

" 'Oh, no. It's his name, at least it's the name Bob's using these days, but, you, bub, never asked Marshal Owens if that man he arrested, if that certain man-killer, if he is sitting in this courtroom today. The state never properly identified my client as the man accused of the slaying. The state has rested its case. There is no case, Your Honor. I request this farce be dismissed.'

"I could have thrown up." Colonel Fountain actually chuckled. "Indeed, I did throw up, a few hours later, after the judge had dismissed the case, apologized to the jury, and instructed me to meet him in his chambers, or I should rather say, the woodshed, immediately."

"What did the county solicitor say to you?" Rex asked.

"Not one thing. Turns out, he and both the defendant and the attorney were old poker-playing cards, and he had asked me, for all intent and purpose, to prosecute the case, knowing that I would make a mess of things. He had not been impressed with my cases. No, gentlemen, he found me to be the idiot that I was. He was right, too. I let a murderer go free, but I learned from that mistake. Since that day, I have lost very few cases, and in those that I did lose, I believe justice was served.

"Justice must be served again, and I believe it will be. Oliver Lee will not go free."

Chapter Four

If I had been disgusted with Las Cruces, I can't describe my disappointment at seeing Lincoln for the first time. To hear Colonel Fountain, Kim Harrigan, and Rex Steele speak of this city, I anticipated a booming metropolis full of wild cowboys and lawmen, only to discover a village much smaller than Las Cruces—indeed, the population numbered barely 350—when we rode in from the southeast on a dreary morning.

Kim read the disenchantment in my face, for he spit out tobacco juice and asked: "Not what you expected, Caleb?"

"Well," I stammered, "it's . . . well, smaller. . . ."

"Like Capt'n Hart's brand?" Laughing, he slouched forward in his saddle.

"I mean," I tried to explain, "there's only one street that I can see."

"Yeah," he agreed. "But a lot's happened on that one street."

To me, Lincoln appeared prettier than Cruces, not as charming as Mesilla. Flanked by piñon- and juniper-dotted hills on one side and what passed for a river on the other, the village lacked the structure of Mesilla and, for the most part, the ribaldry of Las Cruces, although, to hear Kim Harrigan talk, that hadn't always been the case.

As we followed the tree-lined street, muddy from a morning shower, we passed more adobe buildings, and Kim kept pointing out to a spot here and there, like a guide showing tourists around a national monument or something: Juan Patrón used to live there. He might have been the toughest man ever to call Lincoln home. . . . There's where the lawyer from Las Vegas got shot dead. . . . The Kid killed Sheriff Brady and one of his deputies long about here. . . .

Over to my right, he pointed at a vacant lot. "Used to be the McSween house," he said, "before they burned it down and killed him and some other poor souls."

People, most of them Mexicans, stared at us with a certain amount of suspicion, apprehension, until they recognized Colonel Fountain. Then they broke out into an excited chatter, pointing fingers at us, many of them smiling, others calling out salutations to *el coronel.* A plump woman in dirty white cotton and sandals raced out of a hut, carrying something in her outstretched apron, and she stopped in the middle of the street and passed out warm tortillas as we rode by.

I gobbled mine down in a hurry. It sure tasted better than the broiled bacon we had been eating along the trail.

At the far edge of town, the colonel turned his buggy toward a long, rectangular building—the only two-story structure I'd seen in town, unless you counted the round tower of crumbling rocks, a few rods down the street. *Torreón,* Kim called it, built for protection in the early days against Apaches. Horses and buggies crowded the front of the building, so Rex, Kim, and I veered off to the hitching post at the hotel on the other side of the street.

"Rest of the boys," Rex ordered, "take your horses to the livery. Meet us over here at the Wortley. Caleb"—he winked—"let's get us some real grub."

Ravenous, I waited with anticipation. Rex gave a waitress our order in Spanish, and she returned a moment later with glasses of beer for the two cowboys and, to my chagrin, milk for me. Yet when she brought three plates heaping with roast beef and mashed potatoes, I forgot all about wanting that beer. I ripped into the food without bowing my head or muttering a blessing, wanting to savor the taste of the juices, the beef, and the butter, but also longing to fill my shrinking stomach.

Luckily I had wolfed down almost all my food when a tall man wearing an unbuttoned Mackinaw coat and dust-coated black hat entered the Wortley Hotel dining room. Rex and Kim had concentrated on drinking their beers, and were just lifting their forks when the man strode to our table, his spurs chiming.

For once, Rex wasn't grinning. Nor was the man staring down at us.

"Is that what you call guarding Albert?"

"We watched Colonel Fountain all the way to the courthouse," Rex answered.

"I expect you to stick to him like you stick to a saddle. I'll let Salazar spell you now. Least, he follows my instructions to the letter."

His hair was close-cropped, his eyes a deadly yellow-gray—like staring at a wolf, I imagine—

and he sported a thick mustache and goatee, the rest of his face covered with a few days' growth of graying beard. He wore shotgun chaps, tall brown boots, and a large Schofield revolver belted high on his narrow hips. A green silk bandanna hung over a collarless shirt, once red, now faded to pink.

"I'm sorry, Frank," Rex muttered.

"Yeah, well. . . ." My uncle's gaze landed on Kim Harrigan, who sat there silently, his thumb absently tracing the top of the empty stein of beer.

"Harrigan. It's good having you with us again."

Kim nodded. He didn't, I immediately noticed, say: *It's good to be here.*

At last, Franklin J. Hart, my uncle, studied me. "You Caleb?"

"Yes, sir," I managed through a mouthful of potatoes and butter.

"Take after your ma." I had heard that many times before, but back in Missouri I took it as a compliment, yet I found nothing flattering in the way Captain Hart said it.

That was it. Captain Hart turned back to Rex and ordered us outside. Rex briefly considered the last finger of beer or his finger of roast beef, decided on his better judgment, and fished out a few coins from a change purse before hurrying after our boss.

Captain Hart had started across the street, but stopped when he spotted Colonel Fountain, Henry, and two older men, one carrying the cowhide, crossing the street toward the Wortley. With a scowl, the captain spun around and walked back to the hotel porch, pulled a pipe from his coat pocket, and struck a lucifer against the adobe wall. By the time the Fountains and other two men had arrived, my uncle's pipe was smoking, and he looked still to be steaming.

"Franklin." Colonel Fountain set down the wooden dispatch case that seldom left his sight, and held out his hand with what I considered, for a man like the colonel, reluctance.

They shook curtly. "I'm leaving Jesús Salazar with you, Albert," Captain Hart announced. "How long you figure this grand jury deal will last?"

"Barring the unforeseen, we should be finished before the month's end."

"Reckon I can spare Salazar that long."

"There is no need . . . ," Colonel Fountain began, but before he could continue, the man holding the skin stepped between them.

He was a big fellow, raw-boned, barrel-chested, with snow-white hair, drooping mustache, and blowing Dundreary whiskers. "Frank," he said in a rich baritone, "you got to see this here." The old man's knees popped as he knelt with a grunt and laid out the skin, hide side up on the wooden porch. He pointed to the brand and looked up.

"Pigpen," Captain Hart said, reading the brand, which I would have called a ladder or something along those lines. "Oliver Lee's brand."

"That's right," the old man said. His face was red from the sun, his green eyes clear, his teeth yellow, lips cracked. Snorting, he leaned over and turned part of the hide over, revealing the flesh side. Even I could tell the brand had been altered.

"H-Bar," the captain said.

"Dang right," the old man said, and now his ears had turned red. He muttered an oath, much stronger than dang, repeated it, and cursed Oliver Lee long and hard. "That's my brand," he said, and swore again. "Lee's stealing my cattle!" He held out his hand toward the other man, a slimmer version without facial hair except a small, neat mustache. "Help me up, Judge."

Captain Hart looked back at the colonel. "That your case, Albert?"

"There's more. I'd rather not discuss it."

He quickly asked Rex to bundle up the piece of evidence, and Rex immediately obliged.

"Do you plan on staying in Lincoln?" the colonel asked my uncle.

His head shook. "I got work to do. Grand jury ain't open to us no-how." Finally I spotted the trace of a grin, though one I suspect held no mirth whatsoever. "Unless you plan on indicting me, Albert."

"Not this time, Franklin."

"Well, I'll try to see you before you leave. Don't let Salazar get killed on your account. He's a top hand." He looked down at Fountain's son. "This your boy?"

"Yes. Say hello to Captain Hart, Henry. He served with me with the Mesilla Scouts, before you were born."

The boy mumbled something, and Captain Hart turned around, found me, and jutted the pipe stem in my direction. "This is my nephew," he told the older men. "Caleb Hart. Lucas turned him lose on me. Caleb, this big, boisterous no-account is Fred Hutchins. The quiet gent is his brother. We call him Judge."

As we shook hands, the captain puffed on his pipe, looking at Colonel Fountain, who matched his stare. Fred Hutchins started spouting off all sorts of stories, saying he was right pleased to meet me, that the captain was a man to ride the river with, sure enough. Well, I liked Fred Hutchins immediately. You had to like him, much as you had to enjoy Rex Steele's company. I liked his brother, too.

"And the ugly fellow." My uncle's thumb hooked toward Kim, and he introduced him. "Don't know if y'all remember him, but Harrigan used to ride with me back in the mid-'Eighties."

"Sure, sure," Fred Hutchins said, but I knew he was lying as he pumped Kim's hand. "Where you been keeping yourself, Hanrahan?"

"Wyoming."

"Well, it's good to have you back. But, now, if you get tired of working for the captain's wages, the H-Bar is always looking for a good man."

"The H-Bar," the captain told me, without looking at me, "is south of here, but you'd call us neighbors."

Fred Hutchins let loose with a belly laugh again. "Caleb, your uncle here's got more neighbors than a politician on the eve of election. You'll find his brand all over this country."

"The difference is," Judge Hutchins said while winding a handsome gold Waltham Vanguard watch, "Frank Hart only brands his own beef."

Thus the conversation turned to politics, Democrats versus Republicans, honest ranchers and rustlers, statehood or territorial status. Young as I was, this type of talk bored me tremendously, and from the look on Captain Hart's face he felt the same.

Fred Hutchins suggested a drink, and, without waiting for acceptance, he led Rex—the cowhide rolled and tucked underneath his arm—Kim, and Judge Hutchins down the street toward a small saloon. Unsure, I reluctantly decided to remain with my uncle, lest Franklin J. Hart frown upon the thought of blood kin trying to sneak a taste of liquor. That left me smiling dumbly at Henry Fountain, who stared at his brogans.

"It has been a long while, Franklin." The colonel broke the silence.

"Couple of years."

Colonel Fountain tilted his head toward the men as they entered the saloon. "I remember Kim Harrigan."

Now they held my interest.

"Figured you would."

"You brought him back . . . after that . . . incident . . . in Wyoming?" It marked the first time I detected Colonel Fountain struggling for words.

"Sent him a telegraph. He came. He's a good cowhand."

"He's handy at other things, too."

Interest turned to frustration. They kept bandying words, kind of like duelists with rapiers, trying to feel one other out, find their weaknesses, strengths, feelings. Why couldn't they just tell me what Kim Harrigan had done up in Wyoming, and what was he so handy with? That bolt-action rifle in his saddle scabbard?

"Franklin." The colonel let out a sigh. "We have been friends for better than twenty years, since you were riding for John Chisum and later with Colby King. I have fought with you, fought beside you, and I have defended you, and your actions, even when I found myself at odds with your methods."

He waited—I waited—but my uncle made no reply.

"Then let us not mince words," Colonel Fountain said, his tone bitter. I had heard Colonel Fountain angry, always powerful, but never like this, about to lose control. "I am for statehood, Franklin. But to obtain statehood, we must have law and order. Law by the books, sir, not this frontier justice more suited for dime novels or sordid melodramas. The first step is to bring men like Oliver Lee to justice, and I can do that. By God, I will do it. I must do it. By the same token, I will bring anyone who breaks the law to justice. As an officer of the court, I am sworn to uphold the laws of this territory, the laws of our nation." He pointed a finger, almost touched my uncle's chest.

"I saw that look in your eyes, Franklin, when Fred showed you the hide. That was an error on my part. I should have never let him see it. I will bring charges against Oliver Lee, Bill McNew, James Gilliland, Tom Tucker, all of those scum. I will bring down Albert Fall, that thorn in my side, too. They will be charged with larceny of cattle and defacing of brands. Maybe more. Don't try to settle accounts yourself, or you will face my wrath and the wrath of this territory." As Colonel Fountain lowered his finger, I realized he was shaking.

Calmly Captain Hart tapped his pipe against the wooden column. "If Lee's stealing H-Bar beef, that's business between Judge, Fred, and Lee," he said coolly. "Not mine, unless Fred or Judge ask me, and you know, prideful as they are, that won't ever happen. As far as I know, Oliver Lee's never touched one of my cattle. And he knows better than to start now."

The colonel's nod was slight before he turned back toward the courthouse. "Then we understand each other."

"Not quite." Captain Hart waited for the colonel to face him in the hotel's little courtyard. "I don't care one whit about statehood," he continued. "About anything, Albert, but what's mine. In the twenty years I've been in this territory, the law's done nothing but mollycoddle rustlers and killers, and it don't matter who has been in charge, Democrat or Republican, Mexican or Irish, God-fearing or free-thinking, you or the Santa Fé Ring. You can try to change that, Albert, and I wish you luck. But if Oliver Lee or anyone touches what's mine, then they deal with me. Not with the sheriff and not with God. Just like I dealt with Ab Northrup. Just like I dealt with Thaddeus Holliday."

Colonel Fountain's face had turned sad. He pulled his son close, and steered him across the courtyard. Only once he looked back, speaking softly but firmly before stepping into the street. "But at what cost, Franklin?"

My uncle's face hardened, but just briefly.

"I can sleep nights, Albert!" he shouted to Colonel Fountain's broad back.

Chapter Five

Shortly after the Fountains left, my uncle instructed me that I would call him Captain Hart, or Mister Hart, or just plain Hart, and within the hour he had rounded up the crew from the saloon and a mercantile and pointed us on our way to his ranch.

"How're your legs?" the captain asked me before we departed Lincoln.

"A little stiff, but I'll be all right," I answered honestly. Well, sort of honestly.

"Uhn-huh."

Rex came to my defense. "Caleb centers a horse real good, Frank. I been watching him."

"Reckon I'll be the judge of that," the captain said as he mounted his big buckskin.

As you might expect, I wondered what I had signed myself up for, thought perhaps this was the biggest mistake of my life, even churned over the childish notion that my parents didn't love me, sending me here, to this man. Once eager, I now found myself filled with dread, one disappointment after another. Where was all that adventure? Maybe Las Cruces hadn't been so bad, after all. Certain-sure, St. Louis sounded inviting.

We forded the Río Bonito, a mere trickle, and headed east in silence, seven riders on horseback and a Mexican driving a buckboard laden with supplies. Those boxes and bags of grub and staples, I suspected, had brought Captain Hart to town, not to greet me or talk with Colonel Fountain.

The captain rode ahead, naturally, with Kim Harrigan at his side. By my best guess, Captain Hart was explaining things, or the way he saw things, to Kim, so I rode alongside jovial Rex Steele.

"Give you a piece of advice," he told me when we began to lag behind the other riders, for my legs felt more than just a little stiff, and my horse, Chuck, had far from a smooth gait. Even the wagon passed us. "Frank ain't one who likes to wait. We get to a wire trap, he don't like stragglers. He wants everybody to be there, so he can open the gate, shut it in a hurry, and move on. So don't let yourself get too far behind. Let's kick her into a trot for a spell."

Over the next few months, Rex would offer much advice on horses and cowboying, and I learned to listen to him, knew he wasn't telling big windies when he spoke of horses. I tapped Chuck's sides with my boot heels, and we darted past the buckboard, not slowing to a walk until we had caught up just behind the captain.

"Your stirrups too long?" Rex asked. "I can shorten them up at the ranch."

I shook my head. Shorter stirrups frightened me, for, as stiff as my legs had become, as chaffed as my thighs felt, I questioned if I could even pull myself into the saddle with stirrups harder to reach.

"I like them a little long," I said, and that

remains true enough today, though I've learned to adjust them every now and then to ease my joints and muscles. I'm not sure, however, that I spoke the gospel back then, but Rex accepted my explanation and made a comment about the weather. He always had something to talk about.

Ominous skies and a biting wind darkened our mood, at least everybody's but Rex's. Since my arrival to New Mexico, a cold front had moved in. The world, or what had become my part of the world, had grown darker, uninviting, forbidding. There would be breaks in the weather, sunny and almost warm days here and there, but for the rest of that winter and much of early spring, the gloom would hold fast. God had been trying to warn us, I remember thinking months later, of what was about to happen in Lincoln, Guadalupe, and Doña Ana counties, and on the Hart range.

The country flattened as we rode, the piñons becoming scarce, replaced by gnarled juniper, yucca, and bear grass, but predominantly rocks. The setting sun didn't stop us—supper would have to wait—and the wind became more biting as we followed a rough trail on a moonless night through cañons and arroyos.

"I hope your eyes are better than mine," I told Rex.

"Actually Chuck's eyes are better than both of ours," he said, and patted his mount's neck. "So are Galisteo's. And Frank and me have rode this trail many a time. Home is just up yonder."

Sure enough, only minutes later dogs yipped as we crested a hill and descended into the Hart headquarters. The place smelled of horse apples, but I eventually would find something pleasing in that scent. "Manuel," the captain ordered as we dismounted near the main corral, "you and Caleb can unload that wagon in the morn. Not much use in breaking a leg tonight."

After rubbing down and feeding our horses and storing the tack in the barn, the hired hands ambled toward a long, rectangular building of stone and picket slats, while Captain Hart walked alone toward an adobe house, its walls plastered with calcimine, giving it a dull white finish. I waited, uncertain.

"Caleb," my uncle called out, "you come here for a minute!"

He had stopped at the portal, filling his pipe with tobacco. I hurried and stood beside him, waiting, but he didn't speak again until he had taken several puffs on his pipe.

"You'll sleep in the bunkhouse," he said.

"Yes, sir."

"I pay thirty a month and found, but I don't give jobs. I don't give nothing. You work, you listen, or I turn you loose. I told Lucas as much, and he agreed."

"I know." My head bobbed nervously, but I had been practicing this speech since Trinidad. "I want to learn, Captain. I, well, I don't want to be a clerk in some mercantile the rest of my days, so if you see me doing something wrong, you just let me know. You're not going to hurt my feelings."

He withdrew the pipe. "Well, Caleb, the deal with me is I don't rightly care if I hurt your feelings or not."

My stomach soured as those bitter wolf eyes bore a hole through me. I could hear my father talking to me. *Frank can be a hard man, Caleb.*

I felt like I had to say something, and, remembering my father's words again, I said: "I'll ride for the brand, sir."

"You ain't riding nothing yet. You'll work, work hard, but only men ride for me, and, when I think you have the makings, and only then, you'll ride. Tomorrow, you'll help Hobbs, he's my cook. After you and Manuel unload the wagon, you'll muck out the stables, clean the barn, and do whatever Hobbs needs done. You'll earn your keep."

"Yes, sir."

"Like I said, I pay thirty a month and found. Hobbs Wallace is about as good a cook as a body'll find, so you ain't going to go hungry. In exchange for that, you put in an honest day's work. More than that, really, because your last name is Hart. That ain't what I expect, it's what gets done. After a few weeks, I'll determine if you're ready to ride my range. I supply the horses. My riders supply their own saddles."

My face sagged.

"What is it?" the captain demanded.

"I don't have a saddle, Captain. I. . . ."

Grunting, he tapped the pipe against the wall before opening the door to his house. "Come here," he ordered, and held the door for me.

His home surprised me. Oh, you'd have to call the furnishings Spartan, a curtain-top desk against the west wall, cuspidors in every corner, a small table and chairs, all covered, seemed like, with the layer of dust prevalent in this country. A gun rack stood next to the desk, and everywhere I saw pieces of tack, harnesses, bits, even a shovel. Yet I found the house inviting, and thought it had once had a woman's touch: an imported French mirror in another corner, and the crucifix and candles above the fireplace. With his pipe stem, the captain pointed at a parlor chair near the fireplace, the oak frame in need of a good polishing and the brocatelle upholstery ripped beyond repair.

Sitting on that chair was a saddle.

"Best go store that in the barn," the captain said.

Well, I'd know that saddle anywhere, having seen my father work on it enough. A Wyoming stock rig, with steel fork, sixteen-inch tree, tooled *tapaderos* protecting brass-bound stirrups, with thirty-inch skirts, wool-lined. Trembling, I walked over, grabbed the thick horn, and started to pick it up. I turned back toward the captain, just to make sure I had heard him right.

"I . . . I thought Papa finally sold it," I told him. "It . . . it had been sitting in the store for so long."

"Lucas had it sent out here soon as I wrote him that I'd hire you on." He walked to the desk, sat into a rough-hewn chair, and opened a drawer. I thought he might be finding a letter my father had written, but he pulled out a bottle instead, and splashed three fingers of amber liquid into an enamel mug.

"I wonder. . . ." I glanced back at the saddle. "Must have cost him a heap of money. He should have sent it along with me."

Captain Hart downed his whiskey and scoffed. "And let some baggage-smasher ruin it?" Shaking his head, he muttered a small oath. "Not hardly. Or trust it with some kid wet behind his ears better'n a thousand miles? No, Lucas done right." He pointed at the saddle. "Well, take it.

Get that mess of leather off my good chair. Dawn comes early, boy. You best get some shuteye."

I started to lift it, but, spotting some dust, I fished out my handkerchief and wiped off the smudge. For the first time, Franklin J. Hart chuckled.

"You might make a cowhand, after all, Caleb," he said warmly, but I wondered if he would have been in such a good mood if he hadn't shot down that whiskey. "Go on, now. See you at breakfast. And watch for rattlers on the way back to the bunkhouse."

It had to be too cold for rattlesnakes, so I thanked him, expecting him to tell me not to thank him, that he hadn't sent me that saddle, that if I wanted to thank somebody, I'd best thank my father. He said exactly what I had expected, too, but now I realized that Franklin J. Hart wasn't half-horse, half-alligator. He was human. Partly human, anyhow.

As I lugged the heavy saddle across the room, the door nearest the French mirror opened, and an elderly voice called out: "Frank, is that you?"

Well, I'd never seen the captain move so quickly, but he opened that desk drawer and pushed the whiskey bottle inside before I knew what was going on. Next, he shot to his feet, and said, his voice no longer as tough as steel: "Yes, Mama."

He stood there, hat in hand, and I watched, too stunned to move, as the woman stepped into the candlelight. She was thin, like the captain, but I saw little in her face that reminded me of Captain Hart or my father. Stooped now with age, wearing spectacles, her long silver hair pinned up in a bun, she wore wool-lined Alaska slippers and bright-colored flannel robe over a camel's hair sleeping frock.

"Got a late start out of Lincoln," my uncle was explaining. "Didn't mean to wake you."

"Oh, you didn't wake me, Frank. Was reading Balzac. Where's . . . ?"

At that moment she saw me, tightened her robe, and crept toward me, as if she were approaching a skittish horse, fearful I'd gallop away. I wasn't going anywhere, not because of fear, but shock. I try to remember her face, try to paint myself a picture of Anna Elizabeth Hart, but I just can't do it, not with any justice. I remember the voice, remember everything she was wearing—that's the son of shopkeepers for you—but her face still eludes me. Oh, sure, I say she didn't look anything like my uncle or father, but that was through a fourteen-year-old's eyes. Frank Hart had a dark mustache and goatee, his brow constantly crevassed in anger. My dad was grizzled, stoved-up, scarred, old beyond his years. Of course, a kid couldn't find any resemblance.

"Come here, Caleb," she said. "Let me get a good look at you. I never seen you before."

I didn't move.

She stood in front of me with wrinkly-skinned fingers tracing the contours of my face, over my lips, and I saw tears welling in her eyes. One thing I knew for sure: looking at her was not like staring at a wolf, or Frank Hart.

"Oh, yes, yes," she murmured. "I thank God I lived to see this day. You're tall, like my Caleb was. How old are you now? Eleven? Twelve?"

"Fourteen," I managed to answer.

"Fourteen. Oh, my. That's right. I'm forgetful. Well, lean over here, Caleb, and let me give you a good, long hug."

It was my uncle who spoke. "Boy," he said, the authority back in his voice. "Take off your hat, and do what your grandma says."

Chapter Six

"I didn't know ...," I began, but didn't know how to finish. Grandma Anna looked at me lovingly, gave me a kiss on the cheek, and simply nodded as if she understood.

I didn't know ... what? That she lived in New Mexico Territory? That I even had a grandmother? My father had never spoken of her, not that I could remember, and I knew my mother's parents had died when she was in her teens.

"I raised two prideful boys, Caleb." She led me to the dusty parlor chair. "My Caleb, your grandpa, he was a prideful man, too. Went off to fight the Yankees and didn't come home. Died of fever some place in Virginia with Hood's Brigade. Warrant it hurt his pride deep that he died in bed, couldn't get kilt by Yankee ball or grapeshot or nothing like that. But my two young boys became men after that, figured they had to help their mother. And they did ... riding on trail drives, working at ranches, always sending me a little money home. Then your pa got crippled up. It hurts him, I suspect, that he can't take care of his poor old mother. Prideful. But I don't blame him none. I know how hard it is to run a store, to make a living, and he has more mouths to feed than little ol' me. Besides, none of us Harts ever been much for writing letters and such, and Missouri's just too far for an ol' woman like me to travel. I just thank the Lord I got to meet you before I'm called to Glory."

"You live here?" At last, I had completed a sentence, short as it was.

"No." She sniggered. "I ain't the poor ol' mother my boys think I am. Ain't that right, Frank?" The captain grunted a reply. "No, Caleb, I have a little house up in Puerto de Luna. Run the old Grzelachowski store. It ain't much, but it keeps this seventy-four-year-old lady busy. Reckon I've lived up there nigh ten years. Moved from Texas. Frank, now he wanted me to stay with him, but I'd have nothing of that. Reckon I'm prideful, too, and plan on earning my keep till I'm six feet under. You'll have to come visit me sometime. Now, I want you to tell me all about yourself, and my other grandbabies. How is your pa and ma?"

For the next hour, I told Grandma Anna all about my brother and sisters, about the mercantile and St. Louis, about my mother and father, and just a little bit about me. The captain busied himself at his desk, poring over a ledger book, mumbling something underneath his breath every now and then. My grandmother would laugh at my descriptions, and pat my knee. The regrets I had felt about coming to the territory quickly faded away. I even forgot all about my raw thighs and aching muscles.

"How do you feel?" she asked me after far too many stories. "It's a long ride from Las Cruces."

"Good," I answered. "Kind of proud, too. I'm the first grandchild you've ever seen." I could just imagine myself suddenly, back home, bragging on that, tormenting my siblings with that piece of brag.

Grandma Anna's eyes dropped, and she murmured: "Well. . . ."

I knew I had misspoken, and the captain was out of his chair.

"It's getting late," he announced. "You best get back to the bunkhouse. You can talk to your grandma some other time."

Weeks would pass before I would have a chance, a real chance, to talk to my grandmother again, for she left the next morning, after breakfast, saying she had to get back to her store at Puerto de Luna, inviting me to come up and see her when I had a chance, and giving me another bear hug and kiss.

In the meantime, I grew accustomed to ranch life, got to know the other Hart riders, those that were around then, anyway.

Bunkhouses in the winter are mostly empty places, although the captain worked more riders than most. In fact, some of the boys who rode in with us from Mesilla rode out the next day, and I wouldn't see them again until March and April. Other men were camped in the line shacks across the country, from Seven Rivers to the south to Fort Sumner to the north, around the Lava Flow to the west, and practically all the way to the Texas border on the east.

Yes, the Hart range covered a lot of territory.

Like I've said, I've forgotten the names of many of those cowboys. In the bunkhouse at the main ranch that January there were seven men and me.

I've told you about Kim Harrigan and Rex Steele. Manuel—can't remember his last name, if he even had a last name—was the youngest, next to me, with dark hair almost as curly as Henry Fountain's. He didn't speak much English, and most of the time when the captain or Rex or Hobbs Wallace would give him an order, they would talk English and he would answer in Spanish. Since I understood little Spanish back then, the two of us didn't talk much.

Then there were the Sutton brothers, Tim and Earl, both of whom would be the cause of some of the ugliness to come. Them and Slim Reed, but he wouldn't show up till March. Tim Sutton, he was red-headed and freckled, restless I'd describe him as, always went off half-cocked, but about the best hand I'd seen with a lariat. His brother Earl had sandy hair, slicked down with grease, thick mustache, and a little Van Dyke beard. He kept to himself mostly, the exact opposite of his brother, played a lot of cards, and rode off on his own more than the rest. I wouldn't call him a loner— that was Slim Reed, for sure—but he had to be the least friendly of our bunch.

The best man with a horse, next to Rex, that was Dickie Fergusson. I'm not sure he had seen twenty summers by then, and he had dark hair, a clean-shaven face, dancing blue eyes, and loved everything about being a cowboy, as long as he could do it on horseback. He and Rex, now, they were the jokers. I think Dickie was always scheming, and, as rail-thin as he was, I don't think I've ever met a man who could drink so much beer. And tobacco? By jacks, he could beat Kim Harrigan in a spitting contest. He loved to sleep, slept too late most mornings, and would throw down a cup of coffee and a biscuit and had to run to the barn, grab his gear, and saddle up before everyone else rode off. But Dickie Fergusson was a top hand.

So if I haven't miscounted, that leaves only one other man, maybe the most important one in the bunkhouse, that being Mr. Hobbs Wallace. No, there's no maybe to that statement.

Hobbs was probably halfway between forty and fifty, on the chubby side, and favored his left leg when he walked. He had bright brown eyes, a little black mustache, and crooked teeth, a couple of front ones capped with gold. He was the cook, and the captain hadn't been stretching things about his abilities with a cast-iron skillet or Dutch oven. Hobbs liked to say—"You won't lose weight riding for the Hart brand."—which wasn't exactly the truth, but I don't think anyone ever went hungry with him cooking three squares a day.

Hobbs was pretty much my boss during those first few weeks at the ranch. I hardly ever saw the captain. He'd ride off, most times before the sun was up, checking water holes and wells, horse pastures and fences. Can't say I missed my uncle much, though. Things seemed more peaceful, less intimidating, when he wasn't around.

The first day, after Grandma Anna said her good byes, I helped Manuel unload the wagon, and then Hobbs sent Manuel off on some errand while I cleaned the stables and corrals. My legs didn't hurt so awful by noon, because my hands were getting a heaping dose of splinters and calluses. I was mighty glad to hear Hobbs call me in for something to eat.

Outside the bunkhouse, I washed up in icy

water. As I dried my face and hands on a dingy towel, I looked up at the hill on the other side of the main house. The white cross on the hilltop stood clear against the smidgen of blue in the otherwise dreary sky. I hadn't noticed it until then.

"Is that a cemetery?" I asked Hobbs, who stood on the porch sipping coffee.

"A grave," he told me, "but we don't speak of that." Tossing out his coffee, he started inside the bunkhouse, then pivoted to face me again. "That's hallowed ground," he said, shaking a scolding finger in my face. "Don't you go up yonder exploring."

The thought hadn't crossed my mind. "Else there might be another grave there?" I said, trying to be humorous.

It wasn't funny. "We don't joke about such matters," he told me. "Come on, let's eat."

That was one of the few times I saw Hobbs Wallace in a foul mood, or at least somber, and I learned my lesson, tried to forget I'd even noticed the tall white cross. Sure, I was curious, wondering who had died, but I was smart enough by then not to ask prying questions, or disobey orders from Hobbs Wallace.

So I worked. My hands toughened with the chores. Chopping firewood or gathering dried chips for fuel. Breaking ice in the water troughs for horses, dogs, and cattle. Shoveling and sweeping. Mending tack (Kim Harrigan taught me the saddle-stitch). Digging a new privy. Digging another well. Cleaning the stables, barns, and corral. Feeding horses. Forking alfalfa. Running errands for Hobbs Wallace. In short, I did every dirty, nasty, cumbersome, or downright boring job on the ranch. I did the chores no self-respecting cowboy would ever do.

And never once did I complain.

Sometimes I worked with Manuel, digging the well, for instance. More often, I toiled by myself. I wore out one pair of cheap gloves, had to borrow a good pair from Dickie Fergusson. Wore holes in my pants and coat, too, and my $2.25 pair of store-bought boots soon became not only well ventilated in the soles, but got the left heel knocked off. With some glue and an iron screw clamp, I mended that, temporarily.

When pay day came, Kim suggested that I ride to town with him and the boys and get some decent clothes, something that might last.

The captain hesitated. "Figured I'd just send all of Caleb's pay for this month, since it ain't a whole month, to his folks."

"That's fine, Capt'n," Kim said, "and next month you can just send Caleb here home in a pine box with a note to his folks about how he caught pneumonia before he froze to death."

Kim Harrigan was the only person I knew who could talk to the captain like that and get away with it.

"He's worked mighty hard, Frank," Hobbs Wallace added, "and he sure needs some decent duds."

I knew better than to say a word.

The captain grunted, whipped out some greenbacks, and said: "There's ten dollars. The rest I'm mailing to Lucas. Sign your name."

Hoofs sounded, the dogs barked, and we stepped off the bunkhouse porch to see Jesús Salazar trotting down the hill. With a curse, the captain made a beeline for the weary rider.

"I told you to stick with Colonel Fountain," he snapped before Salazar could step off his horse.

Once again, the captain spoke in English while Salazar used Spanish, but I wasn't the only one who couldn't understand.

"What's he saying?" Dickie Fergusson asked.

"Salazar says the colonel and his son rode out of Lincoln on Thursday," Rex translated. "Said the colonel refused to let him ride along."

"I don't rightly care what he said, Salazar," the captain raged. "I give you your orders. Did you come back here because it's pay day." He muttered another oath. "Thursday, you say he left! Today's Saturday!"

Salazar spoke evenly, calmly, and once again Rex translated. "Jesús says he followed the colonel anyway on Thursday, all the way to Doc Blazer's place in Mescalero. But the colonel demanded he go back. 'Tell Captain Hart,' he says the colonel told him, 'that his debt is paid in full.'"

The captain swore again, slapped his thigh with his hat, and shook his head. "Well, it's Albert's hide," he said. "Grand jury's out?"

"Yo no sey."

"Indictments?"

"Yo no sey."

"Dumb greaser," Earl Sutton muttered.

"All right." The captain returned to the porch and finished handing out the wages. A short while later, everyone at the ranch mounted up and rode to Lincoln.

In town, I was much more concerned with buying new boots and a decent coat than with learning about the grand jury. Judge and Fred Hutchins stood talking in front of the livery when we rode in, and Fred waved the captain over. As Kim and Rex steered me to the mercantile, the Hutchins brothers and the captain made their way to the saloon.

I outfitted myself with a fine pair of mule-ear boots, a pine-ridge sombrero, a couple of flannel shirts, socks, underwear, gloves, and a heavy canvas coat with a shawl collar. Of course, the boys wouldn't let me be finished with just that. Rex insisted that I get a pair of britches, striped blue wool with a canvas-reinforced seat, and Kim threw in a piece of supple leather that he said would make a fine pair of chaps. Give him something he could work on during the rest of the winter, he said. They tossed in a couple of silk bandannas, canvas suspenders, and piled them up, along with two air-tights of peaches and a handful of peppermint candy, on the counter.

"Wait a minute!" Dickie Fergusson shouted from the doorway.

"What is it?" Rex asked.

"Ain't he a mite undressed?"

I blinked.

"Why, certain-sure," Rex said. "We'd best fix that, eh, Kim?"

Noncommittal, Kim began to open an air-tight while the elderly man working the counter beamed with anticipation as Dickie Fergusson stepped inside and pointed at the glass case.

"What size would you say he is, Rex?" Dickie Fergusson asked.

"I'd put him at Thirty-Two caliber," Rex answered. "You think that's right, Kim?"

Kim just knifed a slice of peach into his mouth.

Before I knew it, they had dressed me up, throwing away my old clothes, and I stood there—proud, I have to say—from new boots and new hat, bandanna around my new shirt, suspenders holding up my new pants, with a heavy belt high on my waist and a five-inch-barrel Harrington & Richardson double-action revolver holstered on my right hip.

By the way, my friends, I should point out, were sober.

"Why, if he ain't the spitting image of Wild Bill Hickok," Rex told the clerk, who grinned and assured us all that Rex was speaking the gospel.

"Needs some spurs," Dickie Fergusson said as he thumbed brass cartridges into the loops on my new gun belt.

"I got an old pair in the bunkhouse he can have," Rex said. "We need some money for the Bonito."

"Let's settle the tab," Rex added, slapping the countertop. "I feel finer than frog's hair cut eight ways and the need to irrigate."

The total had to come well above my $10, but they wouldn't hear of me paying one dime. My money, I was informed, would buy a few rounds over at the Bonito Saloon. We had cause to celebrate. It was Saturday night, pay day, and the Hart riders had come to Lincoln to tree the town. So, with Kim Harrigan eating peaches from the can with a knife, we crossed the street and entered the saloon, ordering whiskies and beers. A mug slid across the bar and stopped right in front of me.

"Pay the man," Dickie Fergusson said. "For all of us. And drink up."

I didn't get a taste of that beer, though, for Captain Hart stepped up to the bar, followed by the Hutchins brothers.

"Fergusson," he said, "you're well mounted. I want you to ride to Las Cruces, make sure Colonel Fountain got home all right."

"You think he's in trouble, Frank?" Rex asked, then downed both his beer and shot of whiskey in a hurry. The leather hide Kim had purchased at the mercantile hung over his left shoulder.

It was Fred Hutchins who answered. "Thirty-two indictments!" he bellowed. "That's what Colonel Fountain got. He got indictments against that crooked Lee, his gunhand, Gilliland, got charges against every tramp there is that we know is defacing brands and stealing stock. Them boys are up the flume."

"That might just start the ball," Dickie Fergusson said. He drank his beer, but slid the shot glass of whiskey to Rex.

"You ain't kidding," Fred Hutchins said. "When Colonel Fountain walked out the courthouse on Thursday, somebody handed him a slip of paper. It said . . . 'Iffen you drop this matter, we'll be your friends. But iffen you don't, you ain't gonna get home alive.'" Fred Hutchins nodded emphatically.

"Hit the trail, Fergusson," Captain Hart said. He turned, looked at me for just a moment, then walked out of the saloon without comment.

Chapter Seven

That night, it began to sleet, and we sat in the bunkhouse, drinking coffee, wondering about Dickie Fergusson, about Colonel Fountain and little Henry. We hadn't treed Lincoln, after all, hadn't done much but listen to Fred Hutchins rant and rave. Then the captain said we might as well head back to the ranch, that there wasn't much we could do. The Sutton brothers complained, said it was Saturday night and they felt like dancing a jig with a pretty *señorita* or two. I should say they complained later, back in the bunkhouse. You know they wouldn't have said anything along those lines in front of the captain.

Manuel and Hobbs Wallace kept stoking the fire in the Star Windsor stove, but I still felt cold. Cold all the way to the marrow in my bones. It was that kind of night. I sat on a stool near Kim Harrigan's bunk, watching as he worked on my chaps. Earl Sutton darned a pair of socks, and Rex Steele sat beside the coffee pot, thumbing through a three-year-old copy of the *Police Gazette*. Jesús Salazar lay in his bunk, sound asleep. Some Saturday night on pay day, eh?

"You're a pretty handy fellow to have around," Tim Sutton told Kim, just to start up some conversation, to fight off the boredom. "Stitching leather, braiding horsehair."

"I got plenty of practice."

"Rex tells me you cowboyed up in Wyoming." Sutton pulled up a chair, straddled it, and watched Kim work. "I drove a herd of horses to a ranch there one time. The J-Slash-L up on Three-mile Crick. Where did you work?"

Kim punched a hole in the leather with an awl, then slid a string of sinew through it with a big needle. "Last five years," he answered at last, "I was at The Big House across the Laramie River."

Sutton sipped his coffee and shook his head. "Don't rightly know of that one, but, well, I was only up in Wyoming that one time. Good outfit?"

"Bunked in better places, bunked in worse."

"Y'all run, what? Shorthorns?"

"Men." He fished out a brass button, pushed needle and sinew through the hole, and began to stitch it to my chaps. "Bank robbers," Kim went on. "Killers. Horse thieves. Rustlers. Bunco-steerers."

"You worked in a prison?" Sutton straightened. "Not exactly."

Scratching his chin, Sutton settled back into the chair, and took another sip, studying on what he had just learned about the new hand. I thought about it, too, and came to my conclusion a lot sooner than Sutton did, only I kept my trap shut.

"You mean . . . ?" Sutton blinked rapidly, got that look in his eyes he kept getting when he became overly excited. I swear, I beat Tim Sutton in maturity. "You mean . . . you was *in* prison?"

That side of the bunkhouse suddenly became

the prime section of real estate. Even Hobbs Wallace drifted over.

"I been in the Eddy jail a time or two," Rex Steele said without looking up from his magazine. "In Mesilla. Las Vegas, that was the worst. Lost count of the times I been in the El Paso jail."

"Ain't the same," Hobbs Wallace said with a frown. "I been in jail twice, but this is prison."

"Earl served two years in Cañon City, Colorado," Tim Sutton bragged, and started to expound on that before his brother snapped at him to shut up, then cursed up a storm when he pricked his finger with a needle.

"Can I ask you what you was in for?" Tim Sutton asked as soon as his brother stopped cursing and stuck his index finger in his mouth.

"You can ask," Kim answered, concentrating on the chaps.

"Well?" Sutton prodded when Kim hadn't answered.

Finally, with a sigh, Kim looked up. "Said you can ask. Didn't say I'd answer."

"Well, does the captain know?" Sutton demanded, suddenly haughty.

"He knows." It was Rex Steele who answered. "Fact is, everybody knows it was a miscarriage of justice. Kim's an innocent man."

"Of some things," he said, and returned to his leatherwork.

Sleet pelted the roof, the only sound for the next minute until Rex tossed the *Police Gazette* aside, slapped his hands together with a loud clap, and suggested a game of draw poker, which the boys readily accepted, drifting back to the big pine table. I stayed put, but I have to admit my eyes turned away from the dark piece of leather to the rifle leaning against the wall near Kim Harrigan's bunk. It was a battered Brown-Merrill single-shot, older than I was, heavy as a cannon, that fired a 560-grain bullet charged with eighty-five grains of powder. A whole lot different than the Winchester and Marlin carbines the other cowboys owned. My brain concocted all sorts of stories about Kim Harrigan, about Wyoming, and I kept thinking about the conversations I had heard between the captain and Colonel Fountain. Names popped back into my head: Ab Northrup . . . Thaddeus Holliday.

Well, I figured, trying to fight down my suspicions, Kim hadn't murdered anyone. Else, they would have hanged him. Right?

When I looked back at Kim, my mouth turned dry and my stomach felt queasy, for he was looking at me, staring mighty hard. "You want to ask me something, Caleb?"

My head bobbed slightly. "Can you show me how you make that stitch again?" I asked, and relaxed when he smiled.

Dickie Fergusson hadn't come back by Sunday, but no one acted all-overish about it. After all, Las Cruces lay more than 100 miles from the ranch, and the weather remained rough, although the sleet and eventually snow had stopped by Monday morning. Work went on, as did the gossip about Kim Harrigan, whenever he wasn't close enough to hear. By grab, cowboys and cooks have some imagination. Why, you should have heard some of the stories the Sutton brothers and Hobbs Wallace made up about Kim.

Kim Harrigan had been leader of the Hole-in-the-Wall Gang before Butch Cassidy betrayed him, and got him sent to The Big House. . . . He had robbed the Union Pacific at Medicine Bow. . . . He had robbed a bank in Cheyenne. . . . He had run guns to the Sioux during the Pine Ridge outbreak back in '90. . . . He had gunned down two sheriff's deputies in Billings (before Hobbs Wallace informed the originator of that tale, Tim Sutton, that Billings lay in Montana, not Wyoming).

Of course, I can't talk. My curiosity remained, and, while I figured I knew better than to pry into things not my business, I had some wild theories myself. About the silliest notion I got came when I looked up at that hilltop and saw the white cross again, and I wondered if maybe Kim Harrigan had killed someone, after all, and they had buried him here.

Then I shook my head. Kim spent five years in prison in Wyoming, not New Mexico Territory. I didn't know much about law, but I had to think people didn't spend time in Wyoming pens for crimes committed in Lincoln County, New Mexico, and murderers, if they did not hang, served longer sentences than five years.

Well . . . I reckon I know better now, understand that some murderers go free, that not all crimes are punished.

But, to get back to my story, I had other things to think about. That afternoon the captain ordered me and Harrigan to take a wagon into the Capitan Mountains and bring back a load of fence posts. He never said why he sent Kim, and not Manuel, on this chore, but I suspect he had heard the Kim Harrigan stories being swapped over horse apples—which is what most of those stories were anyway—and that he figured it might be best to get Kim away for a couple of days. Out of sight, out of mind, as the saying goes.

I felt eager to get away from the ranch, too, and excited to be traveling alone with Kim. After all, I had never been alone with a man who had been in prison before, and the idea of traveling with an old outlaw sounded downright adventurous.

It took a couple of days to reach the mountains, and we didn't talk much on the ride out. Too cold with the wind blowing, for one reason. Guess I was too nervous, too, despite my excitement. Want to hear another dumb thought? Briefly, and I mean just briefly, I got this notion that the captain had sent us to the mountains so that Kim could murder me and bury me where my body would never be dug up.

That trip marked the first time I saw Mary Magdalene Holliday. That's what I remember most, instead of the smell of sap and sweat as we chopped down trees for posts, or how the cold air burned my lungs. We were nursing our team of mules up a switchback when we heard the cattle, and a couple minutes later she came, driving maybe ten head in all, down the mountain. A brindle steer balked when it saw us, tried to bolt back up the mountain, but this woman jerked her reins, and her horse went to work, blocking the steer's path. They danced a little jig, seemed like, and she hoorahed, waved her hat, and the brindle steer gave up, turned around, and bolted past the wagon.

When she came alongside us, she reined up,

letting the cattle move downhill on their own. She slapped her hat back on her head and spit out a small stream of juice that splattered against the Hart brand burned on the side of our buckboard.

Now, I reckon I just stared there with my mouth agape, because . . . well, for one thing, she had to be one of the most attractive women I'd ever seen. I guessed her age to be maybe twenty, and she had dark hair, long and wavy, hanging from underneath that battered slouch hat, a couple of beauty marks on her lower cheeks, and the blackest eyes I've ever seen. Her skin looked smooth, bronze, and despite the cold, her tan coat was strapped behind the cantle and bedroll. She didn't ride sidesaddle, either, but sat on a big slickfork saddle like a man, Winchester in the scabbard, and I'd never known any woman, except a couple of old ladies in Missouri and my grandma, to dip snuff.

"You ride for the Hart?" she asked, wiping her mouth with the sleeve of a red wool shirt.

Kim turned his head to spit. "Yes, ma'am," he answered. I waited for him to ask her name, because I surely wanted to know, but he didn't. That was bad form in those days.

So I got over my shyness in a hurry. "I'm Caleb Hart," I told her. "This here is Kim Harrigan." Mayhap, I figured, that would lead her to telling us her name.

Instead, she asked: "Hart?"

"Yes," I replied. "Captain Hart's my uncle."

"My sympathy," she said, and started to nudge her big dun horse downhill. Kim stopped her.

"Didn't recognize your brand," he said.

"The association don't recognize it, neither," she said.

"Brand looks kinda blotted."

She hooked a leg over the saddle horn, and laughed. "You are a Hart rider, sure enough." Another spit. "Don't think I've made your acquaintance."

"Been in Wyoming for a good number of years," Kim said, "but I rode for the capt'n back from, oh, 'Eighty-Four, I guess, to 'Eighty-Seven."

"About that time I was in El Paso," she said. "And Fort Davis. And Tascosa. And Tucson. And Yuma. I done some traveling."

"Uhn-huh."

She found her stirrups again, fingered and spit out the remnants of her snuff. "Better catch up with my beef. Nice chatting with you fellas."

"Uhn-huh."

The dun had taken only a couple of steps before she pulled up again, leaned back, and said, grinning widely: "You tell Frank Hart that Mary Holliday's back. That'll fix his flint."

With a tip of her hat, she spurred the dun—yes, she had spurs, too—and the horse exploded into an smooth lope, darting past the rocks and trees, and, to my disappointment, out of sight. I looked up at Kim.

"What did she mean by that?" I asked.

Kim whipped the reins, and the buckboard lurched forward. "Warrant we'll find out once we get back."

"You aim to tell the captain what she said?"

"Got to. I ride for the brand. And my mama raised me better than to disobey a lady's wishes."

"What was her brand?" I asked.

"Couldn't say. Like I told her, looked blotted to me. But I'd bet next month's wages those beeves used to wear Hart brands."

We made camp that evening in the hills, sharpened our axes, checked our saws. Kim made coffee, and he had brought along some canned milk, which proved lucky for us, because Kim's coffee wasn't much better than Rex Steele's. I felt the urge to talk, to learn more about this woman I had met. A woman who rode like a man. A woman who dipped snuff. A brazen woman, strikingly beautiful with dark Spanish features and large breasts straining against her red shirt. A woman Kim Harrigan suspected of rustling.

"You ever heard tell of a woman rustling cattle?" I asked. It seemed hard to accept.

"Some," he muttered.

"Why didn't you stop her, if you think she's stealing the captain's beef?"

He shrugged, preparing the bacon we would broil on sticks.

I considered this for a few minutes. If Mary Holliday was rustling cattle, she wouldn't be alone. Perhaps her comrades had been behind the trees and rocks, drawing beads on our chests, ready to shoot if Kim reached for that bolt-action Brown-Merrill. I shot a glance at my revolver, told myself it might be wise to sleep with it close tonight. Then I came to the girl's defense.

"I don't think Mary Holliday would steal any cattle."

The bacon began to sizzle.

"Could be," Kim said, stirring milk into his coffee.

Holliday. . . . The name hit me like a rock.

"You ever know a man named Thaddeus Holliday?" I asked.

"Nope."

"Well, I heard the captain mention his name to Colonel Fountain. He said he dealt with him. Dealt with him and another man named Ab Northrup." Kim grunted. "I'm just curious. This woman said her name was Holliday. Might be kin."

"Probably so."

"So it could be that Thaddeus Holliday . . . maybe her father, or brother . . . maybe he rustled cattle. Now she's rustling, too."

He reached over and refilled his coffee, set the pot on a flat rock, and chuckled. "Thought you said you didn't think she'd steal cattle."

"Well, I don't . . . but . . . well. . . ." I sat up a little straighter. "I ride for the brand, too." *Sort of*, I thought to myself.

"You're soundin' like a Pinkerton detective." Kim tipped back his hat, his bright eyes reflecting the firelight.

"Well, I'm just curious."

"I bet. She's a handsome woman."

I must have blushed. Anyway, my cheeks didn't feel so cold all of a sudden.

"Maybe," I said, "Thaddeus Holliday and Ab Northrup were part of a gang. Maybe she was part of the gang, too." Suddenly the thought of Mary Holliday being a rustler, a bad girl, appealed to me. Intriguing, at least. My, oh, my, I must have sounded like Tim Sutton.

"No." Kim looked at the bacon. "Like I said, I never met no Thaddeus Holliday. And Northrup made his mark along the Río Hondo back in 'Eighty-Six, 'Eighty-Seven. If you believe that gal, Mister Pinkerton Detective, she wasn't in these parts around then, by what she told us."

I grinned back at him. "Sounds to me like you're being a bit of a Pinkerton detective, too."

His head shook. "Stock detective."

"You knew Ab Northrup?" I asked.

"Not well," he replied. "Now you best let me concentrate on this bacon, Caleb, lessen you want it burnt to a crisp."

I took the hint, read Kim's change in mood. The conversation had ended.

Chapter Eight

"Fergusson's back," Kim said as he eased the buckboard down the road toward the ranch three, four days later. He had to tell me twice, and even then I didn't hear him until he gave me a gentle nudge and jutted his jaw out toward the corral where Dickie Fergusson's blood bay mare pawed the frost-covered ground.

I elbowed Kim back, and pointed my head in the direction of the other ridge, which had commanded all of my attention. Captain Hart stood up yonder, black hat in hand, looking down at the grave underneath that cross. Never had I seen him up there. By grab, I'd never seen anyone there, recalling Hobbs Wallace's explicit instructions that it was forbidden territory, sacred ground. I shivered, and Kim let out a heavy sigh.

This couldn't be good.

It wasn't.

Other mounts, all Hart horses, were tethered in front of the bunkhouse, and no one came out to greet us as we unhitched the team and turned the mules loose in the corral. Kim said we might as well leave the posts we had cut in the wagon, until we learned where the captain wanted them put, and we moved inside with some reluctance. Captain Hart still stood at the grave, a solitary figure, practically a silhouette, against the forbidding sky.

He was sick of repeating the story after umpteen times, but Dickie Fergusson told us, just the same. It had to be my imagination, but Dickie looked older now, weary, just about worn down to the nubbin, and he had been back at the Hart Ranch for three days. Hobbs Wallace brought out a bottle and splashed some into Kim's coffee mug, breaking his own rule that outlawed liquor being consumed in his bunkhouse, and then held the bottle toward Dickie Fergusson.

"Just a small one, Hobbs," Dickie said.

"Hobbs Wallace don't do small." The cook filled Dickie's mug with three fingers of rye.

"Col'nel Fountain's dead?" Kim asked.

Dickie nodded, downed some rye, and shook his head. "Well, I mean, most likely."

He began his tale.

Riding hard, Dickie Fergusson had made it to Blazer's Mill on that first day, Saturday night, and talked briefly to Doc Blazer, who lamented the fact that the colonel had not allowed Jesús Salazar to ride along with him. Even Blazer had pleaded with Fountain, after Salazar had left, to let him send a couple of Indians along with them, but the colonel wouldn't hear of it. That had been Thursday night and Friday morning. Doc Blazer asked Dickie to spend the night, but Dickie said he'd push on, too. He spent a miserable night on the Mescalero range, ran a cold camp, and saddled up before dawn and headed toward Tularosa.

The Fountains had come through there sometime Friday, or so Adam Dieter told Dickie at his store when Dickie stopped to buy oats for his mare. So Dickie began to think, maybe, everything would be all right. Over stout coffee, Dieter informed Dickie that the colonel had said he thought some men were trailing him, keeping just far enough back so he couldn't see who they were. Looked like cowboys, Fountain had said. "You ride careful," Adam Dieter had cautioned the lawyer, tilting his head toward little Henry.

At Luna's Well, Dickie met up with a couple members from the search party from Las Cruces.

Saturnino Barela, the mail carrier from Las Cruces, had chatted with the Fountains in the San Andres, the riders informed Dickie. Fountain had also told Barela that he was being followed, which caused the mail carrier to pause. Barela, it seems, had seen some riders ahead, around Chalk Hill. Cowboys, that's all he could tell about them, because whenever he got close to them, they'd gallop off. Colonel Fountain had then pulled his Winchester across his lap. The hammer, Barela had immediately noticed, was cocked.

"Turn back," the mail carrier had begged the colonel. "We'll spend the night at Luna's Well, ride back to Cruces in the morn."

It had taken a long while before the colonel answered. At least, that's what Barela had said. But Colonel Fountain had made excuses—Henry was coming down with a cold, the weather wouldn't get any better, and the colonel's wife and children expected him home that night. It was Sunday. He didn't want them to worry. So he had ridden on.

When Barela had ridden back to Cruces the following day, he discovered bad sign at Chalk

Hill. Tracks from the colonel's wagon had led away from the road, and Barela had found other tracks, too. Horse tracks. At least three riders. He then worked his horses into a lather getting back to Las Cruces, telling the Fountains what he had found. It was dark when the posse rode out.

I remembered that country, could still picture the vast expanse of sandhills near Chalk Hill when we had ridden out from Las Cruces. We had used oil weed for our campfire because that bush was the only thing a body could find to burn in that strange desert of white gypsum, so fine, so stark, stretching toward the horizon. How easy it would be for a man, or a boy like me, to get lost in that country, I had thought, picturing myself wandering around the desert like Moses.

The search party had camped near San Agustin Pass before getting an early start the next morning, and had covered the miles quickly to Luna's Well. There, they had learned that the Fountains had indeed passed through, and, no, the colonel had not come back Sunday night. That's where Dickie Fergusson had joined the men, and ridden back with them to Chalk Hill.

"John Meadows and Major Llewellyn looked around." Dickie Fergusson's hands trembled as he brought the cup of whiskey to his lips. "I found a couple of empty shell casings beneath a bush. We guessed one fellow with a Thirty-Thirty Winchester had held up the colonel there, then others had caught up with the wagon, turned it off the road about a hundred yards."

Dickie drank. Shook his head. Went on.

"That's where we saw the blood. A lot of blood.

Dried blood, I mean. Soaked down about a foot into the sand."

By late afternoon, they had covered a dozen miles, following buggy and horse tracks. Near where the dunes were red, instead of the white gypsum, they found the colonel's wagon. His wooden dispatch case was busted, and wind had scattered the papers all over the place. That red sand, Dickie said, kept reminding him of all that blood.

"Best not think about that," Hobbs Wallace told him.

With a nod, Dickie continued.

"Major Llewellyn," Dickie said, "he found the note underneath the seat of the colonel's buggy. You remember, the one Mister Hutchins told us about, the one that warned the colonel he'd never get home alive."

Yet there were no signs of either the colonel or his son, but another member of the posse, a fellow from Las Cruces named Branigan, who could read sign as well as Llewellyn or Meadows, found a place where a blanket had been laid on the ground, a blanket carrying a heavy load.

"Colonel Fountain's body," Tim Sutton said, and muttered an oath underneath his breath.

Dickie Fergusson ignored Sutton's comment.

Five miles away, they came to an old camp, Dickie said, where they discovered cigarette papers, matches, and old fire where someone had broiled bacon. I remembered Kim cooking dinner that first night in the Capitans. These men had cooked bacon the same way, broiling it on sticks—the cowboy way, Kim had told me. Branigan and

Meadows also discovered footprints, mostly of men in boots, but one from Henry Fountain's brogan.

"So," I shot out, "Henry's still alive!"

Must have been guilt. Guilt for the way I had treated Henry on the trail to Lincoln. When had that been? Not even a month earlier. In the bunkhouse, I could see Henry Fountain now, cold, scared, his curly hair black and unruly. One of the riders, I recalled with dread, had suggested that I play with the boy, and I had been angered at such an idea. Now, I wished I had shown just a little courtesy toward young Henry Fountain, wished I had invited him to a game of jacks or something.

"Right?" I pleaded when Dickie Fergusson just stared at me. Tears welled in his eyes. "Henry was still alive!" I shouted.

"No." I could just barely hear him. "Well, I mean we really don't know for sure, but Mister Branigan, he figured it was just one shoe, that them road agents had put the boy's shoe on a stick and made tracks to throw us off the scent." Dickie shot down the rest of the rye. "No, the way they saw things, them . . . them. . . ." His head shook. "They'd done murdered the boy already."

Heart sinking, I almost threw up.

"You follow the trail?" Kim asked.

"On toward the Sacramentos," Dickie answered, nodding slightly. "They split up along around there. One horse went over to Wildy Well. The others rode off toward Dog Cañon. We had to camp that night, it snowing, cold, and most of our horses about played out, and us hungry as all get-out."

"Dog Cañon?" Kim Harrigan frowned.

"That's Oliver Lee's range," Hobbs Wallace told

me, but by the way Kim had mentioned the name, he knew that already.

My shoulders had sagged as Dickie Fergusson finished his story.

The colonel's son-in-law, Carl Clausen, trailed the rider that headed toward Wildy Well, while Fergusson and the rest of the boys rode toward Dog Cañon.

"We didn't get far, though. Couple of Pigpen cowboys drove a herd of beeves heading for Wildy Well." Dickie Fergusson sighed.

"Wiped out the trail," added Tim Sutton, who had heard Dickie's tale many times already. "Done it a-purpose."

"Well." Dickie took a deep breath, shook his head, exhaled. "Wasn't much of a trail anyhow, by then."

"What did the col'nel's son-in-law find at Wildy Well?" Kim asked.

"He found Mister Lee. Watered his horse, asked Lee if he'd help them look for the colonel and the boy. All Lee did was cuss the colonel. That's what Clausen told us. Like I said, I wasn't there. Well, we looked around some more, but the trail had gone cold on us, especially after those cattle had churned up the ground, and we were freezing our ownselves. Nothing much to do but give it up, least for now. So they rode back to Cruces, and I come back here."

The Sutton brothers launched into a cussing contest of Oliver Lee. What kind of men would kill a little boy? . . . Lee was a rustler. Judge and Fred Hutchins had proof of that. . . . Captain Hart should string up those boys at Dog Cañon, every mother's son of 'em, drag 'em through cactus, dump their bodies in the White Sands. No one would ever find 'em there. A body could get lost in those hills. . . . Or in the hundreds of caves hidden in the Sacramento range. . . . Probably where Lee had buried the colonel and poor Henry. . . . No, knowing Oliver Lee and Jim Gilliland, they had probably burned the two bodies, fed 'em to the hogs.

I looked around the bunkhouse, searching out Rex Steele, who sat on his bunk, hat pulled low over his eyes, his boots crossed at his ankles. I had expected him to say something. I mean, Rex was always opining about something, but he just stretched out on his bed, oblivious to the commotion. The Suttons now had the floor—I wondered if they always got this animated after hearing Dickie's story. Probably. The Suttons, especially Tim, were excitable boys.

Tim Sutton held out a lariat. "If the captain won't do a thing, I say it's high time we rode out to Dog Cañon ourselves and strung up Lee for what he is!"

"And what's that?"

A draft of cold air chilled me, and, well, Tim Sutton's face drained of color, and the bunkhouse got deathly quiet as Captain Hart closed the door. His spurs sang out, the only noise except for his boots clumping on the floor, until he stood directly in front of Tim Sutton.

"I asked you a question, Sutton."

When Tim Sutton didn't answer, the captain slapped the lariat to the floor, whirled to face the rest of us, his wolf eyes flaming. "Anybody else got something on his mind?" he demanded.

Only Hobbs Wallace had the gumption to speak.

"Colonel Fountain was a good man."

"He was," the captain agreed. "But before you-all make Albert out to be a saint, let me make one thing clear, and I knew him longer and better than anyone in this room. Albert Fountain was a politician first, Mason second, lawyer third. The main reason . . . no, it was the only reason . . . he went after the rustlers and suspected rustlers wasn't for some sense of duty or justice, it's because of Albert Bacon Fall, the attorney for Lee and a bunch of other Texas hardcases who settled here in the 'Eighties. Fall beat Albert in a couple of elections, took away his power, his glory, hurt Albert's pride. That's why he sank his teeth into this matter."

"Fountain helped you a time or two," Hobbs Wallace said. "Like with Holliday. . . ."

"You don't have to remind me of that," Captain Hart snapped, "but Albert Fountain's got three growed boys and lots of friends, lots of Freemasons who can avenge his death if so be their desire. You boys ride for me, ride for my brand. You don't ride for Fountain, and you sure don't ride in some lynch mob, unless I say you do. And I ain't saying that. We got work to do. Ranch work. Not law work. Spring's coming directly, and until somebody steals my beef or hurts one of my riders or tries to grab my range, then we leave this mess to the law, the Fountain family. Forget about Albert Fountain and keep your mind on Hart beef, Hart horses, Hart land." He pointed a long finger at Jesús Salazar. "I give Albert a chance, but he wouldn't let Salazar ride with him, wouldn't let those Apache pals of Doc Blazer ride with him, wouldn't let that mail carrier ride with him."

He snatched the bottle of rye from Hobbs Wallace's left hand and stormed outside. "Albert Fountain dug his own grave," he said before the door slammed shut behind him.

Chapter Nine

For a while there, things returned to normal. I dug post holes and strung two-point barbed wire with Manuel and Salazar, and let me tell you something: digging post holes in frozen ground with a freezing wind whipping your face is one thankless chore. My Harrington & Richardson .32 got quite a lot of use, too, and I chipped off parts of its pretty pearl handle using the butt as a hammer. The revolver's chambers were empty when I did this, mind you, and I only used the gun after the handle of our adze-eye hammer snapped.

Ripped up my hands pretty good one afternoon, too. Just carelessness on my part, one of the hazards of working with the Sears, Roebuck, and Company wire, but I could count my blessings that the captain had ordered two-point instead of Glidden's old four-point barbs. In a mix of Spanish and hand gestures, Jesús Salazar suggested that I ride back to the ranch and let Hobbs Wallace fix me up, but I wasn't bleeding that bad— think it hurt my pride more than anything else, like the day before when Chuck had bucked me off in front of all the boys—so I just wrapped one of my new bandannas over my right hand and shoved the glove back on my left, and we strung up some more fence before dusk.

"Used to be," Kim Harrigan commented that evening while putting salve on my shredded hands and forearms. I cringed from the burns. "You best take it easy in the morn, Caleb," he said. "Don't want these cuts to get infected." I shook my head. The wounds weren't deep, thanks to my coat and shirt. Besides, I had come to the conclusion about why the captain kept working me so hard. He wanted me to quit, expected me to quit, but, well, like my Grandma Anna had told me, we Harts are prideful folk.

"What were you about to say?" I asked Kim as he screwed the lid onto the salve. That's when I read the label: Veterinary Carbolic Salve.

"I'm not a horse!" I complained.

He grinned slightly. "Only thing we got handy, and it serves the purpose." Wrapping my hands and arms with ripped pieces of white linen, Kim went on talking. "Used to be a man could mount his horse in South Texas and ride all the way to Montana without seein' a fence, hardly seein' a person. Then came the wire, and that changed things. Sodbusters fencin' in their crops. Small ranchers fencin' in their pastures. Big ranchers fencin' in their water holes. Things turn nasty when there's fence around. They strung up a drift fence in the Texas Panhandle in the early 'Eighties, practically all the way from Indian Territory to New Mexico. Killed a lot of beef durin' the blizzard back in January of 'Eighty-Six. I hate the thing. And there was a time when the capt'n, he wouldn't ever allowed no wire strung up on his range."

"Times change." It was the only thing I could think to say.

He tossed the jar onto his bunk, and rose, his knees popping. "Yes, sir, they surely do. And ain't it a shame?"

My hands were stiff, swollen, when I tried to throw the slickfork saddle over Chuck the next morning. It took me a couple attempts, but I finally got the rig on and walked my horse out of the corral before tightening the cinch. A few minutes later, here came Dickie Fergusson, saddle and blanket over his shoulder, spilling coffee from his cup as he ran, late as always.

"Hold up, hold up," he said, "I'm coming." He gave up on the coffee, tossed the mug near the gate, and I joined the rest of the boys in laughing.

"Rex," Tim Sutton said, "you got to do something about that boy."

"I'm working on it," Rex replied.

The mood darkened when the door to the ranch house slammed shut, and the captain strode toward the corral. I expected him to head straight over to Dickie, to cuss and berate him about burning daylight, but my mouth went dry when he stopped beside my horse and stared up at me.

"Let me see them hands," he ordered.

I stuck two fingers in my mouth, bit down on the ends of the gloves, and jerked one off, then held my hand toward my uncle, palm up. He grabbed my fingers, turned my hand over, and began unraveling Kim's bandaging job until revealing scratches and scabs. With a sigh, he nodded at my other hand, so I dropped my reins over the horn, pulled off the other glove, and showed him my left hand, which wasn't quite as cut up as the right.

"Might be smarter," he said, "if you wore them gloves you bought."

"I can't get a good enough grip on things with gloves on," I explained.

"Maybe he just don't like wire, Frank," Rex Steele said cheerily.

The captain did not reply. "Well, you're no good to me with hands like that," he said. "Not stringing wire. Manuel and Salazar can finish up today. You stay here, clean the stalls, see what else Hobbs needs done."

Anyway, that's how come I was at the ranch when the Hutchins brothers came visiting shortly after noon that day.

They drove up in a Michigan surrey as I stepped out of the bunkhouse to the sound of barking dogs. After hollering inside at Hobbs Wallace that we had company, I leaned a shovel against the wall and stepped off the porch to greet them.

"'Afternoon, bub." Fred Hutchins set the brake. "Is the bossman around?"

"He's at the house," I answered.

Hobbs Wallace had stepped into the threshold. "Any news about the colonel?"

"Nah. Democrat papers are spitting out a pack of lies, saying the colonel was running away from his missus. But I brung some more evidence against them rustlers. Sonny?" He nodded at me. "You mind fetching that hide in the back and laying it on the porch here? Me and Judge will run get Frank."

I climbed into the back, found the hide rolled up in the seat, dragged it out, and, with Hobbs Wallace's help, tossed it onto the porch. As we unstrapped and unrolled it, Mr. Hutchins released the brake and rode up toward the house. The captain must have heard the dogs, because he stepped outside, pulling on his coat, and stood there talking with the brothers a few minutes, then climbed into the wagon and rode back to the bunkhouse.

"Somebody's a right poor hand with a running iron," Hobbs Wallace said, and, for the first time, I really noticed the hide. Wallace turned the skin over and, shaking his head, mumbled something I couldn't understand. By that time, the Hutchins brothers and the captain had stepped off the surrey, and Fred Hutchins was spitting out his story.

"One of my boys found this over in Tularosa day before yesterday," Mr. Hutchins said. "Turn that hide over, bub . . . let Frank here get a gander at it."

I lifted the hide up so that the captain could read the brand before the rustler went to work.

Well, I didn't even have to look at the brand because I knew the hide, could see that brindle steer back in the Capitan Mountains, could picture Mary Magdalene Holliday on her fine dun horse, blocking the steer's retreat, pushing it back down the mountain while Kim Harrigan and I sat in the buckboard, watching.

"At the Irishman's?" my uncle asked.

"Yes, sir. My boy, he asked him about it, but you know that fellow. Says he bought it from a guy he'd never seen before. Same story he's been telling for years now. We ought to tar and feather that man, run him out of the valley on a rail." He nodded emphatically.

I let the corner of the hide drop, and slowly rose.

"That's your beef, Frank." Judge Hutchins spoke now, his voice steady.

"I know that."

"Lucky our rider grabbed that hide before the Irishman could burn it, after butchering your beef," Judge said, but Captain Hart made no reply.

"Well," Fred Hutchins began, "you can bullyrag these vermin only so many times, and, if the threats don't take, it's time for action. Lee's been rustling my cattle. I got proof of that. Now somebody's stealing your'n. I reckon it's time we took care of matters."

When the captain remained quiet, Judge Hutchins said: "Isn't that why you brought back Harrigan from Wyoming, Frank?"

"He's a good hand," the captain said after a moment.

"This is Oliver Lee's handiwork!" Fred Hutchins boomed. "I know it. . . ."

"You don't know a thing, Fred," the captain snapped. "Have you been to Lee's place, asked him?"

"I got better sense, Frank. I don't want to wind up missing like Colonel Fountain."

"If you're scared, take a dozen riders with you. . . ."

"You got no call to say I'm yellow, Frank. Got no call at all. You can let a few squatters and rustlers take a beef every now and then, but not all of us got as much cattle as you do, Frank. Judge and I . . . and a good many of us association members . . . we can't afford to lose any beef. And I've fought rustlers, fought Indians, fought you Johnny Rebs. Now, sir, you best withdraw that remark or I'll fight you, Frank. I might lose, but I'll fight you just the same."

The captain struck a match against the wall and brought out his pipe. "You're a brave man, Frank. You, too, Judge." He held the match to the pipe, got it going, and took a long pull before speaking again. "I'm just not convinced Lee's behind all of this, not by a jug full."

"Well, I am," Fred Hutchins said. "And someone's stealing your cattle now, Frank."

Judge cleared his throat, and, as was his habit, began winding his pocket watch. "The law of this territory is failing us. I was behind Albert pursuing his case, but consider those results. Albert's dead. His son is dead. Murdered. Their bodies buried God knows where. Oliver Lee and the rest of those scoundrels are still free. Free to rustle. Free to kill. You rode with John Chisum, Frank. You rode with Colby King. You know what must be done."

"Did your rider get a description of the person who sold this steer?" the captain asked Fred Hutchins.

"You know the Irishman's memory. Only description he got would describe half the men in southern New Mexico."

"We need to do something, Frank," Judge implored. "This isn't like you at all. Waiting? We can't afford to wait any longer."

"Yeah." After another puff of smoke, my uncle nodded. "All right. Let's see if we can't get some of the other association ranchers together Saturday, in Lincoln. We'll get an idea of how much stock we're losing."

The brothers climbed back into the surrey, and

the captain thanked them for bringing the hide to his attention. "One thing you ought to know, Frank," Judge said. "I've asked Slim Reed if he would consider looking into this matter. Whether or not you join us, I'll be riding to El Paso shortly to learn his price."

The captain didn't say anything, just smoked his pipe, and the Hutchins brothers disappeared over the hill.

Silence.

We stood there, I don't know how long, until Hobbs Wallace asked the captain if he wanted any coffee. The head just shook, and Wallace grunted something before limping back inside, shutting the door behind him. I considered the shovel and the chores awaiting me in the corral, then took a final gander at that brindle hide.

A mighty torment. That's what I was feeling. I kept seeing Mary Holliday, recalling Kim Harrigan's remarks that those steers she was herding had once worn Hart brands. On this dusty porch floor lay proof that Kim had been right. Only . . . this was a young woman, a beautiful woman. Then, there was the captain, blood kin, and right was right. Finally I heard the echo of my father's voice.

You ride for the brand.

I cleared my throat, doubting the wisdom of such a move when I found those yellow-gray eyes boring a hole through my soul. He didn't say a word, just stared, waiting.

"I . . . uh . . . well, sir . . . I . . . I think . . . I mean . . . maybe . . . but . . . you see . . . I think . . . no, I know . . . who stole that. . . ." I pointed at the hide, swallowed down bile, and made myself look into those wolf eyes again.

Slowly the captain withdrew his pipe. "I know," he said, and stepped off the porch. Whether he meant he knew about Mary or he knew that I knew, I could only guess.

"Thanks, Caleb," he said, and I watched his back as he walked away without another word, climbing up the hill until he stood beside the white cross, then swept off his hat, and bowed his head.

Picking up my shovel, I gave him some privacy and went back to work.

Chapter Ten

What happened at that meeting of cattlemen, who all came, what the mood was like, I can't say. Fourteen-year-olds weren't privy to such information, and the captain rode out to Lincoln that Saturday morning alone. I do remember that he didn't return to Hart headquarters until Tuesday, and, when he asked me to unsaddle his gelding— ordinarily Captain Hart didn't trust anyone with this chore—I smelled whiskey on his breath.

During the captain's absence, I had learned that Kim Harrigan indeed had given him Mary Holliday's message. What I didn't do was ask for any details, what the captain had said, how he had sounded, those kinds of things. I knew Kim pretty well, or thought I did, and, if I had asked, he'd have just told me to mind my own business.

Two days later, Dickie Fergusson almost knocked over the captain on the bunkhouse porch that morning when, late as usual, Dickie ran out to the barn to fetch his gear and catch up with the other boys in the corral. My instructions that day were to wait in the bunkhouse, and I expected to get a bunch of orders from Hobbs Wallace, but he had disappeared. When the captain walked inside, I leaped to my feet, almost spilling my coffee.

I felt fear.

"How're your hands?" he asked while pouring himself a mug.

I looked at them before answering. "Mending," I said. "Reckon I'll be ready to swing a hammer or. . . ." My mouth wouldn't co-operate, so I just shut it, and waited until the captain tested his coffee.

"Well, won't be no need in that." He abruptly tossed the mug into the wreck pan. The clattering of the tin unnerved me even more, and Captain Hart put his hands on his hips and gave me a long stare.

"You done good work," he said, and I straightened up a little, for my uncle and compliments weren't on a first-name basis. "Didn't complain, even when you tore up your hands stringing that wire. Rex said you center a horse real good, and I seen as much myself. Chuck can be a mite bronc'y, but you never showed no fear mounting that chunk. Hear tell you got bucked off a few days ago."

Silently I cussed Tim Sutton and Rex Steele for their big mouths, but all I told the captain was: "Yes, sir."

"And what did you do?"

"I got right back on."

He nodded with approval. "That's right. That's what you do. Your pa'd be proud of you."

I considered thanking him, but decided against it.

Outside, I heard Rex and the boys jeering Dickie Fergusson, followed by the thunder of hoofs as they rode off. Silence returned, and the captain and I just looked at each other for what seemed like a good half hour but only lasted less than a minute.

At last, Frank Hart cleared his throat. "Caleb," he said. "Men ride for my brand, and you're a boy. Blood kin, that don't matter. You're still a boy. You got the makings, kid. Fact is, I think you might make a real good cowboy. And maybe in a few years, maybe then you can work for me."

My legs almost buckled, and I couldn't stop the tears from welling. He was firing me. Firing me? Letting me go. After all the work I had done, never once complaining, never shirking my duty, keeping my saddle clean, following instructions to the letter and seldom having to be told how to do something twice.

"Don't you go bawling on me," he snapped, and his long finger pressed against my chest. My lips trembled, but I managed to dam the tears. My head bobbed, or at least I guessed it did. My stomach soured—that I knew for sure, no guessing to it—but I faced my uncle like a man. No crying, not in front of him.

"It ain't you," the captain went on. "Ain't a thing you done, it's just the timing is all. Lucas and me ain't that close, but he's my only brother, and I ain't gonna get his oldest boy killed on my account. This country's about to boil over. That brindle steer ain't the only Hart beef that's been rustled and . . . and . . . that . . . well, it ain't just . . . Holliday. Harrigan found some of my stock over in Los Portales with the brands altered. I done some math, and I got to put my losses at better'n fifteen percent. To rustlers. Now, I'm a fair man, Caleb, don't mind if some family kills one of my cattle if they're hungry. Don't mind the sheepherders. Don't mind a squatter here and there, as long as they remember that they're only there by Franklin J. Hart's grace. Most of them do. Others don't. So there's gonna be more blood spilt, and, well, I think it's best if you'd be somewhere else."

He waited, and I managed to nod my head again and tell him: "Yes, sir."

"I got business in El Paso," he said. "You'll ride with me there. I can put you on a train, grubstake you to a ticket back home."

My head shook timidly. "No, sir."

He stared hard, but I summoned the words. "I recollect the deal being that, if things didn't work out here, I'd find work elsewhere." It comes to mind now that I must have sounded like my uncle. "Be easier on my folks. Reckon I'll just look for a job in El Paso, or thereabouts."

"Suit yourself." Maybe the words don't seem like much the way I say them now, but by looking at Captain Hart that morning, I knew he approved of my decision. "We'll leave in an hour."

I guess he also knew I'd need time alone. Typically the captain didn't burn daylight, and we could have ridden out right then. I didn't have much to pack. I was glad Hobbs Wallace had made himself scarce, because, as soon as the door slammed and I stood in the bunkhouse alone, the dam burst, and my tears flowed.

Since the ranch was practically deserted, there would be no good byes. I couldn't even find Hobbs Wallace anywhere, not that I looked hard. They all must have known the captain's plans, which is why everyone made themselves scarce. I contemplated leaving a farewell note, but decided that writing would just make me cry even more, so I saddled up Chuck and met the captain a short while later.

We made it to Mescalero that first night and camped in the pines. Doubt if we said a dozen words. The following day, we rode through Tularosa and on to La Luz, then moved south, staying in the valley, the Sacramento Mountains to the west, the harsh outline of the distant San Andres glimmering in the east, pointing our way toward Tres Hermanos. Harsh country it was, rugged, windy, oppressive. I spied a few red steers grazing, and smoke rising somewhere in the Sacramentos, but made no comment.

The wind whipped my face, cracking my lips. On we rode, forgetting about noon, riding silently, slowly, conserving our energy, and our horses', as we made our way through the desert.

I spotted the riders first. Well, I think I did, for the captain hadn't said anything or looked toward the rising dust. They loped our way, at first indistinct figures at that distance, slowing when they were perhaps 200 yards away. Two men, one on a gray horse, the other riding a sure-footed sorrel.

When my uncle reined up, I followed his example. He unbuttoned his coat, pushed the tail behind his gun belt, and I felt uneasy. When my hand dropped beside my holstered revolver, he snapped under his breath: "Keep your hand away from that pistol." He couldn't have even seen me move. Naturally I obeyed, and nervously fingered the reins, waiting, watching, barely breathing.

The two men, still mere shadows, stopped, and slowly my uncle lifted his gloved right hand in a friendly gesture. The two talked things over among themselves before kicking their horses into a walk while the captain rested both hands on the big saddle horn. Once they stopped a few rods in front of us, the man riding the sorrel raised his hand.

"'Afternoon, Hart," he said.

"Lee." The captain's head bobbed slightly. "Gilliland."

I could feel my heart pounding, realizing we were this close to Oliver Lee and Jim Gilliland, two men suspected of killing the Fountains, two men indicted for rustling. Rough men, they were, with bearded—though only their thick mustaches looked permanent—and sun-bronzed faces, Winchester rifles in the saddle scabbards, and Colt revolvers snug on their hips, within easy reach.

Although his face looked hard as iron, Lee seemed younger than I had envisioned, narrow-hipped, broad-shouldered, wearing a big crowned hat similar to the ones I had seen atop Buffalo Bill Cody's likeness in advertisements for his Wild West and Congress of Rough Riders of the World. For a cowman, not to mention a suspected man-killer and thief, he was nattily dressed, wearing pin-striped trousers—no chaps—tucked inside fancy-stitched boots adorned with large-rowel spurs, a tailored white shirt with an embroidered De Joinville scarf loosely fastened around his paper collar. His jacket was a double-breasted cardigan. Take away the spurs and the Colt, and he could have passed for any of my father's business associates back in St. Louis.

Gilliland, well, he was another matter. Unkempt he looked, though also younger than I had imagined, wearing dark colors so worn it became right hard to tell where the clothes began and the dirt ended. Pale blue eyes blazed underneath a battered, black hat, and, though he slouched forward in the saddle, I noticed he kept a thumb hooked in his gun belt, right close to that big revolver.

The horses snorted, and the captain gave his a little more rein, letting it chew on a patch of grass. Oliver Lee threw one leg over the saddle horn, and tipped back his big hat. The men paid me no attention.

"Been a mild winter," my uncle said at last, and Lee considered the sky. Gilliland's gaze didn't leave the captain for a moment.

"Could use some more moisture," Lee said.

"Reckon so." Captain Hart also studied the sky momentarily, and I found myself looking for some sign of rain or snow, but for once detected only fading blue. "Much cattle as you're running."

The trace of a smile appeared behind Lee's ragged beard, but it had to be a humorless one. "Well, Hart, not all of us control the Pecos . . . and the Bonito . . . and the Hondo." He pointed off to the west. "Been putting pumps in at all my wells," he said. "Steam-powered. That's progress for you. Cost me an arm and a leg, but my beef won't be thirsty, rain or no rain."

"Had any trouble with rustlers?"

Lee shook his head. "They know better than to steal from the Pigpen."

"Used to know better than steal from the Hart," he said.

"You might should deal with that, then."

"Reckon I will." Straightening in the saddle, the captain reached into his pocket. With a swift motion, Gilliland's right hand darted for his Colt, but my uncle just stared at him, moving deliberately, and withdrew a pipe and a pouch from his inside pocket. "Care for a smoke, Lee?"

The young cattleman shook his head. "Don't use tobacco, Hart. Don't drink, neither. I promised my ma."

Captain Hart nodded, and filled his pipe. "Too bad about Albert Fountain," he said softly.

Lee unhooked his leg, and stood in the stirrups. There was an edge to his voice when he spoke again. "He was nothing to me."

They stared at each other for a long while, then Lee laughed a bit and stretched his arms. "Besides, I heard that he run off to San Francisco, maybe Mexico. Took the kid with him."

"I heard that, too." The match flared against the captain's thumb, and he held it to the pipe, then tossed it aside. "And it's a lie."

The wind picked up, but that wasn't what chilled me. For what seemed an eternity, I held my breath, waiting for the men to draw their weapons, for the fury to be unleashed, but the moment passed, and both Lee and my uncle seemed to relax a bit.

"We're both Texians, Hart," Lee said, his voice pleading somewhat. "Shouldn't find ourselves on opposite ends of this fight, if it comes to a fight. I've left you alone, and that's all I ask from you, and the association."

"If you leave me alone. . . ."

They waited.

"I saw a Pigpen brand on a hide back in January," Captain Hart said. "The deal was that hide belonged to H-Bar beef. Last week or so, I saw another hide. The deal there was it was on one of my steers. And I've seen some other examples of men handy with running irons . . . on Hart beef."

Oliver Lee simply nodded in agreement. "The problem with accommodation branding, Hart," he said, "is that anyone can cheat a bit, or slap another man's brand on a cow and accuse that man of rustling. You should know that better than anyone in the territory, Hart. After all, I remember when you took care of Ab Northrup."

"I remember that, too," the captain said. He removed his pipe with his left hand, keeping the right one free. "But the deal with me is . . . I ain't never killed no kid."

It was Jim Gilliland who laughed, and I mean to tell you it was ugly, sinister, more bark than cackle. He sat straight in his saddle—he must have stood six-foot-four—shook his head, and spoke in a cruel voice, sunlight reflecting off a gold-capped tooth. "You mean the Fountain boy? He had a bean-eatin' ma. Back in Texas, we'd call that kid a half-breed, and give a medal to the man who. . . ."

My uncle's right hand gripped the butt of his Schofield, and he said in a deadly whisper: "Ride off now, Gilliland. Or fill your hand."

I must have sat there trembling in the saddle, too scared to do a thing, my eyes darting from Gilliland to my uncle. Seconds ticked off, and Oliver Lee broke the deadly stillness. "Go on, Jim. I'll meet you at Loco Well."

"I ain't a-runnin'," Gilliland said through clenched teeth, his hand gripping his Colt.

"No one said you are," Lee said again, placating. "Just ride. Hart and me, we're just talking, you see, finishing our conversation. Ride on, Jim. I'll meet you up yonder."

The horse exploded forward, and I about lost my seat as Jim Gilliland galloped between my uncle and me. That man could ride just about anything, I figured, and it took me several seconds before I could calm down Chuck, who wanted to lope after the gray horse. When I did regain control, Gilliland had disappeared in a trail of rising dust, and the captain and Lee were talking again.

"You've done much worse than kill a kid, Hart," Lee said. "Now me? I've never killed a kid, neither. And I think maybe ol' Fountain got tired of licking his wounds, run off to Mexico or California. His family's got friends and law dogs from all over, they've been wandering through this part of the country . . . and I haven't tried to stop them. No reason to. They've dug up stones, and nobody's found no body. Nothing. I suspect that lawyer and his boy are still alive."

"You got your suspicions," the captain said. "I got mine."

"But that's all they are, Hart. Suspicions. Why don't we ask the boy there? He ain't had a chance to toss in his two cents. What about it, boy? You think they'll ever find the bodies of that lawyer and that kid?"

Chapter Eleven

A mighty uncomfortable feeling turned my gut squirrelly as I looked into Oliver Lee's chiseled features. At first, I figured the captain would come to my defense, arguing that I had no say in the matter, being too young for such talk, but he just sat there, chewing on his pipe stem. I stared at the smoke—anything to avoid Oliver Lee's cold, dark eyes—from the mountains, and I don't know why I said it, why I even thought about it, but I remembered the Sutton boys talking in the bunkhouse all those weeks ago, so I pointed to the Sacramentos, where Jim Gilliland was riding.

"I don't know." I wonder how I actually sounded, if my voice cracked in terror, or held steady the way I'd like to remember it being. One thing I do know for sure—I made myself stare back into the bottomless pits of Lee's malevolent eyes. "Those steam-powered pumps of yours, why, I guess you have to burn a lot of wood or coal in those fireboxes. I reckon . . . why you could burn a couple of bodies to dust in those things."

Well, Lee's granite face wasn't so hard now. It was probably just my imagination, but he looked a little green, not so steady, and out of the corner of my eye I also caught the fraction of a smile on my uncle's face.

Lee turned to the captain, glaring long and hard. "If somebody's stealing your beef, Hart, you best look closer to home." Now my uncle stiffened in the saddle. "I ain't slapped my brand on any Hart beef. Never stole an H-Bar cow. If you leave me alone, I leave you alone. Same with the Hutchins boys. By thunder, I got enough problems to go looking for more fights. That hide you saw, the H-Bar changed to look like the Pigpen, that wasn't my doing. I got no fight with you, Hart, and you got no fight with me. You got my word on it."

Oliver Lee rode pretty fair, too, like he had been born to the saddle, and galloped off to the west, chasing Gilliland's dust.

After that, it seemed like Captain Hart felt the need to talk, because he opened up—well, opened up as much as I reckon he would allow himself to—over the remaining miles to El Paso. I learned a lot about him, letting him tell the stories, and they were the bona-fide truth, not like the stretchers Rex Steele could jaw on and on about. I just let him talk, too. Of course, after so many years and my sun-baked brain addled from mounting too many bronc'y horses, it's hard for me to separate what the captain told me during the trip to El Paso, and what I would learn later, from other sources, but I suspect it's high time you understood a little more about Franklin J. Hart's background.

He had hired on with the Chisum brothers in 1872, and drove a herd of Chisum's beef to New Mexico Territory the following year. Along about 1875, John Chisum traded for some South Spring

River property, and before long Chisum controlled about 150 miles of the Pecos River. Captain Hart—and another 100 cowhands, including Rex Steele—rode for Chisum's Rail brand, but the captain decided to go to work for another rancher, Colby King, in the spring of 1876.

"By then I had a . . . well . . . never mind. The Chisums were fair men in many ways," the captain told me, "but they must have been running eighty thousand head of cattle and they was stingy with every last one of them."

On the other hand, Colby King didn't mind one of his hands slapping his own brand on a maverick, here and there. By jacks, that's how Colby King had gotten his start. It wasn't rustling, you see. If a stray calf didn't appear to be following a branded mama cow, well, some folks figured that calf was free for the taking. Now that would lead to some trouble in later years, here in New Mexico and practically all over the Western ranges, but it was policy in the early days. So the captain started his herd, got some land that wasn't controlled by Chisum or King, began building something. Building a name for himself and, though he didn't know it at the time, carving out an empire, a legacy.

No, the Hart Ranch didn't dominate Lincoln County in those days. Fact was, few people ever paid notice to the captain. He rode for Colby King while slowly proving up his own place, a rawhide affair at first, and kept his nose out of the Lincoln County War. Wasn't his business, the way he saw things, more like a feud between money-hungry merchants. That's not to say the captain just sat back and watched the bloodshed in those rough, violent times. No, Frank Hart spilled some blood himself. Colby King, you see, sent the captain along as the C-K-Connected representative to join Colonel Fountain (who was a major then) to ride with the Mesilla Scouts and stamp out the rustling ring operating in Kingston, Hillsboro, all the way over to Silver City. That's how my uncle earned his rank as captain. He helped bring John Kinney in, got his name in the papers, earned a heap of respect.

In 1883, Captain Hart stopped drawing his time from Colby King, hired some of his own cowhands, including Rex Steele, and acquired more range for the growing numbers of Hart beef.

"Figured it was time to be my own boss," he said. "We had four, five really good years. Then came the drought."

Ranching's a gamble. Reckon I don't have to tell you-all that. The captain had good water, and he also had good fortune. That's more than you can say about the Chisums. Big John had been pestered by debts, lawsuits, rotten investments, not to mention rustlers and bad luck. How does that saying go? Cow poor? Well, that pretty much describes the Chisums. When John died of cancer in Arkansas in 1884, the Jinglebob Ranch began to fall apart. I guess the drought finished things off, because by the time "the big die-up" ended in 1892, there was hardly a thing left of the Chisum empire.

Texians had flocked to New Mexico in the 1880s. They took advantage of the Homestead Act and the Desert Land Act, staking claims, scraping out ranches, or trying to raise chickens and crops. There was talk about a railroad from El Paso to White Oaks. Big times. "The big die-up" ended most of those dreams. Cattle weren't the only things to perish during that long drought.

"Some folks called me a bloodsucker for what I did," Captain Hart told me. "But I got called a lot worst. Didn't hurt my feelings none."

What he did is what any gambler or savvy businessman might have done. He took over those failed farms and ranches, added to his range.

"Wasn't pleasant," Captain Hart recalled. "Water holes dried up. Air got rancid with the smell of rotting cattle. All I did was build up my holdings, not my stock. The beef I'd add later, after the drought broke. Reckon I took advantage of other folks' misery, but, if things hadn't turned better, I would have been dead broke, probably dead."

Droughts end, of course, but just a year later, the Panic of '93 struck. Ironic, it is, how the silver bust that drove my father to the brink of ruin added to his brother's fortunes. More ranches failed, more farmers gave up, and the captain's empire grew. By the winter of 1894, the Hart range covered what once had been Chisum territory, and before that Apache land. It stretched from Seven Rivers to just north of Fort Sumner. I doubt if a man on a good-bottomed horse could have seen it all in one summer.

"I been called the King of the Pecos. Well, they called John Chisum the same thing, and look what it got him. I'm still cow poor," he said, and, in a rare display for Frank Hart, he laughed. "But it's my land. My cattle." His humor had vanished in an instant. "Ain't nobody taking nothing away from me." He spit.

We were squatting by a fire, just a short ride from El Paso, broiling bacon the cowboy way. All this time I had known better than to ask any questions, though sometimes I wanted to. I didn't want him to stop talking, and figured there was a pretty good chance his silence would return if I butted in. Or, maybe, just maybe I was just too scared to interrupt the captain.

Now I made myself ask him something.

"Do you think Oliver Lee killed Colonel Fountain?"

He answered with a shrug, and I shot out another question.

"Do you think he's stealing your cattle, or H-Bar beef?"

The look he gave me was one of incredulousness. "He says he didn't."

"Well, yeah, but. . . ."

"He give me his word, Caleb. That means something to a man out here."

He reached inside his coat pocket and pulled out his pouch of pipe tobacco, then cursed when he realized he was out, that he'd have to wait till we reached El Paso in the morning.

"Lee said he ain't stolen my cattle, or Fred and Judge's, and I believe him. Now, did he have a hand in killing Albert and the boy? I wouldn't put it past him. But he better be smarter than to rustle my stock. He was right, too, about one thing. Accommodation branding don't always work."

I knew I'd sound like an idiot, but my inquiries hadn't shut him up yet, so I fired off another one: "Just what is accommodation branding?"

The captain laughed again as he forked bacon onto our plates, shoving one in front of me.

"Some folks might consider accommodation branding a gentleman's way of rustling," he said.

Back in those days, I learned, roundups were done as group efforts, ranchers and cowboys helping each other, being neighborly. If the association recognized your brand, you could take part in the roundup. So, if Rex Steele happened to find a calf trailing close behind a fat heifer wearing an H-Bar brand, he was obliged to slap an H-Bar brand on the calf.

Yet a man might not have sound judgment in such matters. He might figure the calf wasn't following the cow at all. Might convince himself that the calf was sired by his own bull, or that that mama's brand had been defaced.

"But isn't that sort of how you got your start?" I said, and felt stupid, thought Captain Hart might flatten my nose with his plate.

"Lots of cowmen got their start with a wide loop and a hot iron," he said, surprisingly calm. "I figure I'm fairer than the Chisums ever were. Sometimes I don't even mind a poor cowboy being a bit faulty in his judgment with accommodation branding. It's the outright thieves, the rustlers, the killers, them's the one that face my wrath, my judgment."

I swallowed, shivered a bit, but made myself ask the question. "Like Thaddeus Holliday?"

Those wolf eyes landed on me, stuck to me, and my lips trembled as the captain chewed his bacon.

"Where'd you hear that name?" he asked in a dry voice.

It was my turn to reply with a shrug.

"Holliday shot down Colby King. I ain't lost no sleep over Holliday departing this earth."

The captain didn't speak more about that, but Rex Steele would fill in the holes some while later. Colby King, Rex told me, had cut down on his holdings, too, sold off most of his cattle and a lot of his land during the bad drought of 1889–1891. At age 70, he figured it was time to take things easy. When the good rains came again in 1892, it brought back rustlers, too. A man of principle, King wasn't about to lose what beef he had to thieves. He rode into Thaddeus Holliday's camp, and Holliday shot him dead. What happened after that, well, even Rex wouldn't speak of such things, so I'd have to wait even longer till I learned the whole story.

Briefly, and I mean very briefly, I thought about asking the captain about Mary Holliday, who she was, but, well, better judgment—or perhaps fear—quashed that bit of curiosity.

Instead, pushing my luck, I asked: "And what about Ab Northrup?"

He spit again, fished out the tobacco pouch, and muttered an oath underneath his breath, cursing his forgetfulness. "You hear a lot of names," he said as he toyed with the empty leather pouch.

I waited.

"Northrup was a rustler, as big a thief as Pat Coghlan, that Irishman over in Tularosa, only twice as bold. Northrup burned a Hart brand over one of his own steers. Then he accused me of rustling his beef. That's what Oliver Lee meant when he said anyone could slap a Pigpen brand over the H-Bar, and he's right. Northrup filed suit against me, wrote letters to any newspaper that would print them, tried to cheat me, soil my name. Nobody believed him . . . well, not many anyway . . . and he went right on rustling and lying."

Now, he looked again at me, the flickering

flames dancing in his eyes. He spoke just once more that evening before pulling up his soogans and drifting off to sleep. Spoke evenly, softly, without emotion, four words that kept me up most of the night.

"Till I stopped him."

As I feared, that ended Frank Hart's gabfest. We rode the next morning in silence, and I blamed myself. All that prying, especially about the names that fed my curiosity, Ab Northrup and Thaddeus Holliday, had shut him up.

The captain had told me something, told me a lot, during those long days and nights on the trail. Yet, as we trotted into town, I realized the captain had told me nothing. Not really. Oh, now I knew how he had acquired his vast holdings, how he had come to New Mexico Territory as a thirty-a-month cowhand, how he had carved an empire for himself with luck, sweat, and the iron Hart will. I knew he had ridden with Rex Steele while working at the Chisum Ranch, and I knew how he had met Colonel Fountain. Yet I knew nothing about him, personally. Nothing at all. I didn't know who was buried on that hilltop at ranch headquarters, although I suspected it was Colby King. Nope. I didn't know one really important thing about my uncle.

As we rode into El Paso, it struck me with more than a touch of sadness that I probably would never know.

Chapter Twelve

If ever there was a Sodom in this part of the country, it had to be El Paso in the 1890s. I must have counted a half dozen gunshots as we rode into town. Everywhere you looked, people crowded dusty streets and boardwalks while black smoke from the smelters and locomotives hung over the city of 10,000 (with even more than that living across the river in Juárez) like something out of a Charles Dickens novel. A church bell chimed eleven times, echoed by the bells in other missions, all of them straining to be heard over banjo and piano music blasting out from grog shops and dance halls. Bet your boots I rode mighty close to the captain.

Back in August, John Wesley Hardin had been shot dead while shooting craps at the Acme Saloon, and a flock of gents and ladies in derby hats and parasols stood in front of the building, fingers pointing inside as if they were visiting a tourist site. Maybe it was. The trial of Hardin's killer, John Selman, was scheduled to begin in a month or so.

In the Tenderloin district, other ladies, and I use the word loosely, whistled at us from their upstairs porches or windows, and invited us up to see their wares.

Paying them no heed, we kept riding.

I was mighty glad.

Finally we sat in our saddles in front of the noisy depot, the captain working his jaw, me quaking in my boots while trying to look brave. Captain Hart mumbled something, but I couldn't understand him, and he swung his horse around and mentioned something about attending business first.

I felt mighty glad to get away from the depot, too.

Down went McGinty
To the bottom of the sea.
He must be very wet,
For they haven't found him yet.

That's what they were singing, at the top of their lungs, when I followed Captain Hart into Fort McGinty. It wasn't a fort, although it did have a brass cannon out front. A couple of . . . well, "irrigated" . . . singers tried to coax the captain into singing with them, but he shoved them aside, knocked one drunkard onto his buttocks, though that didn't stop the others from their out-of-key merriment, and I followed him into a dark saloon.

Mayhap some of you-all recall the McGinty Club. This wasn't a real club or fraternal organization like the Masons and such. Mostly promoters, I suspect, folks who pushed for music, progress, city improvements, but mostly manly endeavors such as boxing, bicycling, and baseball. And drinking beer.

The red-mustached bartender drew two massive schooners and slid them across a mahogany bar in front of the captain and me. That marked the first time a beer-jerker ever paid me any attention, and the captain didn't object.

Cigar smoke, sweet-smelling but sickening at the same time, clouded the saloon, but somehow my uncle found who he sought. After tossing a coin on the bar, he hoisted his beer and made a beeline to a corner booth, me trailing him, sloshing suds and beer, and arriving with a half-full schooner, leaving a nickel's worth of draft on the sawdust floor.

A slight, leathery man in Mexican denim sat alone, nimble fingers rolling a cigarette, a pouch of Bull Durham on the table next to a greasy fork and a half-eaten can of potted tongue, an empty mug, and a nickel-plated, ivory-handled double-action Colt .44. In most Western towns, ordinances prohibited the carrying of firearms within the city proper. If there ever was such a law in El Paso, nobody paid any attention to it, not even the local constabulary.

He wore his dark hair, flecked with gray, close-cropped, and was clean-shaven in a saloon full of facial hair. Not only that, those denim duds of his would have prompted a fight back on the Hart Ranch, for if I had learned one thing during my brief stay in the bunkhouse, it was that a cowboy wouldn't even be buried in jeans and such, clothes worn by farmers and miners, men who worked in the dirt, not horseback. On the other hand, I'm not sure any Hart rider would have challenged this man.

When he looked at me, I felt as if I were staring into Death.

The captain had slid his wiry frame into the

booth, giving me room, so I sat down, too, and took my first taste of beer. I found it bitter, but smiled at this milestone. Another man appeared as if by magic, nodded at my uncle, and stood there waiting.

"What are you drinking?" the captain asked the man in denim.

"Tom and Jerry," came the answer, a nasal voice, with traces of the deep South.

My uncle sipped his beer, and I tried mine again. Moments later, a steaming mug arrived in front of the man in denim, and the captain handed the waiter a greenback.

"Slim Reed." Captain Hart made the introductions. "This is my nephew, Caleb Hart."

Slim Reed gave me a curt nod and fired up his cigarette.

"I'm here at Judge Hutchins's request, but you know that already," the captain said. "The Southeastern New Mexico Stock Growers' Association has agreed to hire you as a stock detective. Two hundred dollars a month. Fifty dollars for each rustler who is convicted in a court of law, or a hundred dollars for each man, a known thief, who leaves the territory, one way or the other. The agreement is for three months. Then the association will talk over how things have gone."

Sipping his fancy drink, using only his left hand, Slim Reed nodded, then set down the mug, and picked up the cigarette, still smiling. This kind of contract—one not written on paper, not by a jug full, not even sealed with a handshake—made me nervous. Nervous and sick. I was fourteen, green as they come, but I knew what this deal meant. After a moment, Reed blew a smoke ring and looked at me. "What do you think, boy? That sound like a fair deal to you?"

Now, I was getting sick of being asked questions by men like that. I didn't like Slim Reed, not one bit. Liked him even less than Oliver Lee, or feared him more than I feared Lee. Yet I had listened to the captain's words, listened closely, like a fellow hearing a man strike a bargain with the devil. A couple of things had hit me. One was how the captain had said a $100 bounty for each man—he had emphasized man—that left for parts unknown. Man. Like Slim Reed wasn't to touch a hair on Mary Magdalene Holliday's pretty head, which made me glad, although I was probably imagining things. The second thing that grabbed my attention was the price structure. A reward of $50 for each conviction, but an additional $50 for rustlers who simply disappeared.

Anyway, what I said to Slim Reed was this: "By what you charge, killing's more prosperous than doing things legal."

Laughing, he set the cigarette aside and lifted his mug. "Slim Reed gets results. The law don't."

By now, I had lost interest in my first beer. It didn't taste that good, anyhow, and my mouth felt full of bile. With shaky hands, I managed to push myself out of the booth.

"Does Slim Reed disgust you, boy?" said Reed, finding his smoke.

I didn't care for how he spoke of himself in the third person, either. Without thinking, I answered—"Yes, you do."—and left.

Well, I didn't know what to do, on my own, so to speak, as I left Fort McGinty. I mounted Chuck, and somehow followed the streets down the hill until I reached the depot again. After tethering Chuck to a hitching rail, I sat on a bench, stared at my boots, and waited. I can't tell you what I waited for; I just sat there like an oaf. Fifteen minutes later, a locomotive pulled a dozen cars down the tracks to the depot, spitting out smoke and cinders, and I closed my eyes, hearing the din of voices as folks piled off the train.

When my eyes opened, Captain Hart sat on his horse, next to the hitching rail, staring down at me.

"Well?" he said.

Unsure of how to reply, I rose. He had promised me money for a train ticket, which I had refused, but at that moment I had two silver dollars to my name, and only a month's wages coming to me, some of which I'd have to mail my folks. No matter if I stayed on in El Paso or rode west looking for work, I needed a grubstake, at least my $30 in owed wages. Yet, being a Hart, I didn't feel like mentioning this to the captain.

"You need a job?" he said.

"I . . . uh. . . ." Did he plan on recommending me to someone in town?

"I pay men thirty a month and found." I couldn't believe what he was saying as he launched into his speech. "You'll work, Caleb, work hard because I don't give jobs. I don't give nothing. You ride for the Hart brand, you do what I say, or I turn you loose. I got a decent cook in Hobbs Wallace, so you ain't going to go hungry. In exchange for that, you put in an honest day's work. More than that, really, because your last name's Hart. That ain't what I expect, it's what gets done. I supply the horses. My riders supply their own saddles." His goatee jutted out toward my sorrel horse. "Looks like you got a pretty good saddle."

"Yes, sir," I said. Still uncertain, I stuttered: "I . . . I . . . I . . . thought only . . . men rode for the Hart brand."

"That's right. But I figure any kid who'll stand up to Oliver Lee or Slim Reed. . . ." Tipping back his hat, he chuckled. "You turned white as a new saddle, boy, but you showed grit. Any kid like that's worth taking a chance on." He pulled the hat back down and, gripping the saddle horn, leaned forward and barked: "You want the job or not?"

"Yes, sir. I surely do, Uncle . . . I mean, Captain Hart!"

"Then mount up. We're burning daylight, and I need to buy some pipe tobaccy before we leave this. . . ." Well, you don't need to hear what he called El Paso.

Back we drifted toward Hart range, only not the way we had come. Instead, we rode east and northeast, camping the first night at Hueco Tanks on the old Butterfield line, then crossing the Salt Flats and through the Guadalupe Mountains, riding up to Seven Rivers.

We met the first Hart rider at the line shack on Four-Mile Draw. Land here was dry, desolate, and I doubted if it would support many head in the wettest of years. The line rider was a man of color named Old George, white-haired with a glass eye, and he seemed mighty happy to have company, especially the boss'.

They talked about cattle, about the weather. Old George hadn't even heard about the Fountains, but the news didn't surprise him. The captain, however, didn't have any interest in repeating old news.

"We lost any head down here?" he asked.

"Mild winter," the old-timer answered. "Gonna be a wet spring, too. Or so my bones tell me."

"Don't mean natural causes," Captain Hart said. "I mean. . . ."

"I know what you mean, Capt'n. Not enough head to keep a rustler interested down here. I ain't talked to a body in a coon's age, sir, but, well. . . ."

"Well, what?"

"I spied some riders here back two weeks, pushin' a dozen beeves . . . toward Eddy, I suspect."

"How many riders?"

"Three." He refilled our cups with chicory so bitter it made me appreciate Rex Steele's coffee. "When I rode toward 'em to say howdy, one reined up and fired a shot over my head. Gave me the impression they weren't sociable, so I let 'em go on. Ain't ready to get killed, Capt'n, not even for you, sir."

Captain Hart nodded. "That's smart thinking, George."

"Well, I don't reckon them boys got them cows from any of my pastures. Else I'd have sent word to you." Old George paused to carve a piece of plug tobacco with his pocket knife. "Might have been H-Bar or Rockin' R beef. Might have been Hart beef from up north of here. Might have been honest cowpokes who took me for one *mal hombre*."

"You recognize the riders?"

He tapped his glass eye with the point of the knife blade. That I'll remember to my dying day. If I had turned white talking to Lee and Reed, there's no telling how pale I got hearing that *click-click-click.*

"No, sir. Too far for me to see their faces really." After folding the blade and shoving the tobacco into his mouth, he continued: "But I'd know that horse one was ridin'. My one eye ain't that bad, especially after a body takes a shot at me with a repeatin' rifle. Big dun horse. Good stock. And he appeared to have dark hair and was wearin' a red shirt. That's about all I could tell, though."

Well, he didn't need to say any more. The description might not have meant a thing to the captain or Old George, but it sure painted me a mighty clear picture.

Mary Magdalene Holliday.

We criss-crossed our way through other Hart pastures, talked to more Hart riders. Can't say I learned much about my uncle during those days, for his reticence had returned, but I did see a lot of country, and for the first time really understood, or thought I did, the scope of Hart territory. I also learned that, indeed, rustlers were plaguing the captain. Most likely the riders and beeves Old George had seen had come from the grazing land along the cap rock west of Mescalero Ridge, and the cattle had been not Rocking R or H-Bar, but Hart beef.

"Too much country for just a handful of line riders, Capt'n," one of the men told him. "Need some help."

"Yeah," was all the captain said.

I guess Captain Hart had seen and heard enough, because we turned east, to my disappointment. My hopes were that he'd show me all of his land, that I'd get to visit Grandma Anna up in Puerto de Luna, but instead we swam our horses across the Pecos River near Roswell and met up with Kim Harrigan, to my surprise, near Blackwater Draw.

"Who's the new rider?" Kim smiled as he swept off his hat to scratch his bald head.

A grunt was the captain's reply. He had been in a foul mood since Seven Rivers. "The association's hired Slim Reed," he said.

"Heard of him."

"He's heard of you."

When Kim frowned in disgust, the captain spit. "Yeah, well, I don't care much for Reed, neither, but the association don't always listen to me, and he did a right tidy job on the Canadian River back in 'Eighty-Five, in San Miguel County in 'Eighty-Nine, and along the Picketwire in Colorado, year before last."

"Not that tidy," Kim said dryly. "At least, not in Texas."

"Yeah." Captain Hart wiped his mouth with the back of his hand. "Be that as it may, Old George spotted three men herding beef a few weeks back. Turns out it was Hart beef, and they wasn't Hart riders, neither." His tone hardened as those wolf eyes locked on Kim Harrigan. "I'd like to keep Reed off my land, if you're up to the job. Reed can earn his money helping the H-Bar and them other fellows east and south of Hart range. Ain't got to be like the Northrup deal, but things need to be fixed, Harrigan. Fixed teetotaciously."

"All right." Spitting out the remnants of his tobacco quid, Kim pulled on his hat. "I come across an old camp in Deadman Cañon where some cattle had been held. Pretty good spot, too. And they left some runnin' irons and lariats. You like, I could bide my time, see if they come back."

The captain nodded his approval, but warned: "They took a pot shot at Old George. Don't think they meant to do nothing more than scare him off, but if they come back, things might get ticklish. You need someone to ride shotgun for you?"

As he considered the question, Kim leaned back and smoothed his mustache. At last his head bobbed slightly, and his reply about knocked me out of my saddle.

"Could use a good man. How 'bout Caleb?"

Chapter Thirteen

I fully expected the captain to say absolutely not, but it must have been that Hart pride again. Me being blood kin, he couldn't let on to one of his hired men that I wasn't up to snuff for something like this. I'm right sure he didn't want to put me in harm's way—by grab, that's why he had first told me I needed to light a shuck back home—but I reckon he trusted Kim Harrigan's judgment, knew Kim would keep me safe.

"Your choice," Captain Hart told Kim, and spurred his horse eastward, leaving me alone with Kim Harrigan and his Brown-Merrill rifle.

For the rest of March, I followed Kim Harrigan from pasture to pasture, line shack to line shack, surviving mostly on brackish water, snow melt, stale crackers, and beans. Now and then, Kim would drop a jack rabbit with his rifle, and once he shot a mule deer, which was mighty fine eating. Lots of times, our coffee was nothing more than boiling water poured over burned grain.

"What's the matter?" he asked one night.

I laughed. "All this beef, and we're practically starving to death."

He chuckled, too. "Eatin' your own cattle'll make you sick, Caleb. Don't you know that?"

"So will eating your fixings."

"Never claimed to be no Hobbs Wallace. You could have ridden out with your uncle."

"Some nights I wish I had."

Those times I enjoyed, bandying words with Kim when he felt jovial. Plenty of country we covered, but usually turned up at Deadman Cañon, where Kim had found what he suspected as a rustlers' camp. It had a natural corral, which the rustlers had fortified, and Kim pointed out the sign, where they had roped the cattle, dragged them to the fire ring, and branded them with running irons. Three men, he said, and I thought about Old George and the three riders he had seen down south of here. I thought of Mary Holliday, but I didn't tell Kim of my suspicions. I couldn't tell him.

"You think they'll come back?" I asked, hoping he'd say we were on some fool's errand, waiting here.

"I wouldn't," he said. "Rustler gets careless, he gets caught. Gets caught, he goes to prison, or something more permanent. But these gents left behind some tools. Either they've retired, got scared off, or they figure this is too good a hideout to quit."

"I hope they've retired," I remember saying, and the look Kim gave me is burned in my memory, like he knew exactly what I was thinking, or hoping, like he felt the same way, too, but for a totally different reason.

At that time a bunch of things were happening in southern New Mexico. Friends and big political figures had brought in Pat Garrett, slayer of Billy the Kid, to find out who had killed the Fountains, and the family had hired Pinkerton agents to help with the investigation. In Tularosa, Slim Reed killed a Mexican caught with one cow and calf, altered Circle 7 brands, and no bill of sale. The dead man was called Carlito Quintana, and the story went that his name had been on the list of suspected rustlers the association had given that miserable assassin.

"There's one hundred dollars," I said bitterly.

Kim didn't say a word.

Most of the news we picked up came from other line riders and Hart cowboys combing the brush and cañons for cattle during roundup. On occasion we'd meet up with some traveler, preacher, or homesteader, and trade for real coffee or air-tights, but mostly conversation and news. When some peddler gave us a week-old copy of the *Río Grande Republican*, I mean to tell you, that was like striking gold. We read that till we knew it by heart, including the advertisements, and only reluctantly used it to light a fire when the false spring ended.

Old George's bones had told him it would be a wet spring, which proved as accurate as an *Almanac*. Wet—and cold.

Usually we rode together, but, after a couple of weeks, Kim figured I knew the country well enough to hunt jack rabbits for supper. I'd shoot them with my pistol. Yeah, he had a lot more confidence in me than I had in my own abilities.

"Hands up!" the voice called, like a raven's kaw, and, jitterish and stupid, I didn't listen. Instead, I slapped for my .32. Don't know what I was thinking, for I could have been shot out of the saddle. Instead, I wound up with another injury, painfully slamming my palm against the Harrington & Richardson's hammer, then jerking my hand away, shaking it wildly, yipping like a kicked dog.

Mary Magdalene Holliday kicked her dun from the mesquite thicket, laughing so hard she almost fell off her horse. My face flushed, and I stopped the wild flailing and tried to give her my meanest stare. Of course, when I spotted the Winchester carbine cradled in her arms, my eyes widened.

"You ain't no gunman, Mister Hart." She pulled on the reins, and spit out tobacco juice.

"Well . . . you could get killed pulling a stunt like that."

"So could you. Had I been a man-killer, you'd be dead by now. Next time, Caleb, you best listen. Might not be me with the Winchester."

She remembers my name. That's what I recall thinking, and suddenly my hand didn't hurt so much, nor my pride. I looked behind me, scanning the land, wondering if Kim Harrigan were nearby, hoping he wasn't.

"Still riding a Hart horse, I see," Mary said. "That's a pure-dee shame."

All of a sudden, I got angry, angry with Mary Holliday, maybe for shaming me so. Being a Hart, I felt the need to defend my uncle. "What do you have against the captain anyhow?" I snapped.

Her dark eyes hardened. "Everything," she said. A long silence followed before she said: "For one, he hanged my husband."

"After . . . after he killed Colby King," I blurted out.

She spit again, and swore underneath her breath.

"You are a Hart. Next time, reckon I'll just shoot you."

That only made me madder. "Like you shot at Old George?"

Turning her horse around, she shoved the rifle in the scabbard. "I wasn't shooting at him, Hart. Else I'd have hit him."

"An old man, a good man," I said with contempt. "You'd shoot a harmless line rider with a glass eye."

"He rides for the Hart brand," she said, her bitterness besting my own. "He ain't nothing to me."

I had to blink away the vision of Oliver Lee, saying the same thing about Colonel Fountain. She was riding away, back into the mesquite, in the direction of the rustlers' camp. I started to call out to her, couldn't find the words, before panic struck me, my anger disappeared, and I yelled at her to stop. When she paid no heed, I spurred Chuck hard, ducking my head, leaning in the saddle, cutting through the mesquite, and catching her in an arroyo.

"Wait up!" Still she rode on, only stopping after I bolted past her and turned Chuck sideways, blocking the path. After reining in the dun, she wouldn't look me in the eye, just sat in the saddle, staring at her saddle horn.

"You best stay clear of Deadman Cañon," I said.

Judas! I told myself. I was betraying the captain, turning my back on Kim Harrigan. Guess my emotions went on a rodeo, a little like Kim's, jovial one minute, taciturn the next, haunted, bitter. At first, I had been right pleased to see Mary

Holliday, alone, even over my embarrassment, but then we had started arguing, which brought me shame, and now fear. Fear for her life.

"I don't know what you're talking about," she said, still not looking at me.

"Don't play me for a fool, Mary," I fired back. "Kim found your camp. Found the running irons. You and your men ride back there with Hart livestock, and you'll land in jail. Else in a grave."

"Like I said, I don't know what you're talking about."

"You're a rustler. A thief. But I'm. . . ."

"I only take what's owed me, Caleb Hart." She spit out the words like venom.

In exasperation, I moaned. "I'm trying to save your life. Kim Harrigan's waiting for you-all in that cañon." I pointed toward the place. "I don't want you to wind up like that Mexican Slim Reed . . . killed . . . or the Fountains or Ab Northrup. . . ." Well, I didn't actually know what had happened to Northrup. I paused, then made myself say it: "Or your husband."

"It ain't my camp," she said, nudging the dun forward. I reined Chuck aside to let her by.

When she was gone, I just sat there, waiting, letting Chuck graze. For a number of reasons, I hated myself. I rode for the brand now, but I had just warned a rustler. More than that, I had hurt Mary Holliday. Eventually I kicked Chuck into a walk, no longer interested in hunting rabbits, and skirted through the brush and cañons for a good half hour, in a daze, dreaming about what I should have said, what could have happened. I could have spent a fun afternoon with Mary Holliday, could have gotten to know her. I imagined us underneath the shade trees, picking at a jack rabbit I had killed and cooked, saw her lying on her back, a straw in her mouth, humming a pretty tune. Saw me stroking her curly black hair, staring into those mesmerizing Spanish eyes.

Then I heard the bawling of cattle.

My throat went dry. Carefully, slowly I pulled the revolver from its holster, and made Chuck lunge up the embankment. That was pretty green, too, because I came right into view of the man herding the beeves. He pulled up hard, and his hand shot down for his rifle. I just sat there, frozen, gun in my bruised right hand as about a dozen cows and calves walked past me.

The rider's hand hung beside the saddle scabbard. "Hart?"

Through the dust, I suddenly recognized the man, and awkwardly shoved the Harrington & Richardson back into the holster. Kicking the sorrel into a trot, I rode out to greet Earl Sutton.

"I thought you drew your time," Sutton said. Sweating despite the chill, he glanced over his shoulder. A second rider had appeared on a ridge, pausing until Earl Sutton took off his hat and waved him over. The man rode a blood bay gelding, a big one, and the horse covered the quarter mile in no time. Even before he reined up, I knew it was Earl's brother.

"What are you doing here?" Tim Sutton asked.

"Working," I answered boastfully. "What brings you boys out this way?"

Earl Sutton started to answer, but Tim spoke first. "It's roundup time, boy. Ain't you heard?"

"Cattle are getting away from us," Earl pointed out, and spurred his horse.

"Come on, Caleb!" Tim called to me, and I leaped at the chance to drive cattle.

Earl took the point while Tim and I rode drag. When one cow bolted toward the mesquite, Tim and his big blood bay cut it off and pushed it back into line. He reminded me of how Mary Holliday had worked the brindle steer back in the Capitans all those weeks ago.

"Thought you went back to Kansas," Tim said. He spit out dust before pulling his neckerchief over his mouth and nose. I did the same.

"Missouri," I corrected. "No, the captain gave me another chance. How are things back at the ranch? How's old Rex? And Dickie?"

"Fine, fine." He stood in his stirrups and looked around, then Earl pulled up, letting the cattle move past him. The brothers looked at one another, and in some unspoken signal Tim tipped his hat, told me it was good seeing me again, and loped to the front of the herd. I couldn't wait till I was that good a cowboy, reading men's minds, knowing what to do. More than fair, too, I thought, changing the point and drag positions so you didn't always eat dust. I hoped they'd let me ride point, even for just a little while.

"You alone?" Sutton asked.

I wasn't really listening, so I nodded, then asked: "Where are we taking the herd?"

He pointed a gloved finger up ahead. "Little cañon a mile or two from here. We'll hold them there till the crew gets here."

"Sounds good," I said, but then it didn't sound good at all, and my stomach soured. We were headed for Deadman Cañon. The Sutton brothers were rustling Hart beef! Maybe they were Mary Holliday's partners.

Another thought sent a chill up my spine. They'd kill me there, bury me so my bones would never be found. I'd vanish like the colonel and little Henry. Deadman Cañon would earn its name.

Never been much of a poker player. Earl Sutton must have seen my ashen, frightened face, because he reined up with his left hand, drawing a long-barrel Remington revolver with his right. As he thumbed back the hammer, a bullet buzzed over my head.

His face masked in pain, and instantly Earl Sutton was gone, cart-wheeling over the back of his horse, firing the big .44 into the dirt. As gunshots echoed, the cattle stampeded, and I thought I heard Tim Sutton curse. Chuck bucked for a handful of seconds before I calmed him down, and somehow got my bearings. Earl Sutton moaned, face up on a bed of prickly pear, his left shoulder drenched in blood, the cattle pounding their way east. Next I spotted Tim Sutton, rifle in both hands and reins in his teeth, galloping straight toward me. Maybe he thought I had shot his brother.

Another bullet kicked up dirt in front of Tim's horse, and only then did I realize I held the Harrington & Richardson in my right hand. I don't remember pulling it, but I saw myself lift the .32 and jerk the trigger. That caused two things. Chuck started bucking again, and Tim Sutton forgot about his brother and decided to save his own hide. Without slowing his horse, he turned north, spurring wildly. A rifle boomed again from the hills, and I let out some strange growl or howl, something.

Next thing I knew, I had spurred Chuck and was loping after Tim Sutton. Ever read *Ivanhoe*? That's what it brought to mind, me, some knight with a lance, charging on horseback in a joust, chasing the coward, Tim Sutton.

Yep, I didn't know what in blazes I was doing.

Tim Sutton, now, there was a horseman for you. I felt the .32 pop in my right hand, and it's a miracle I didn't put a ball in Chuck's brain. Didn't come close to hitting Tim Sutton or his mount, and Sutton pivoted in the saddle and snapped a shot with the Winchester.

I didn't care. On a galloping horse, not caring to aim, he shot as poorly as I did. Chuck was a pretty good runner, but I can't say I made up any distance on Tim Sutton. Briefly, to the west, I spotted the outline of another rider loping in. All I could see of him was that he rode a paint horse. He reined up, took in what was happening, turned that paint around, and loped back toward the sinking sun.

What I would have done had I caught Tim Sutton, I don't know. Standing in my stirrups, I chanced another shot, the wind whipping my face.

I don't know what happened, if Chuck stumbled or just turned bronc'y on me. Maybe, I'll even concede, my stirrups were too long. Anyhow, the next thing I knew, I was leaving the saddle, my left shoulder slamming into the sorrel's neck, the Harrington & Richardson spinning from my hand. My left arm crashed into the rocks, a distinct *snap* followed by a crushing blow to the back of my head.

I never lost consciousness, just lay flat on my back, eyes clenched shut, head pounding, hearing hoofs thundering in the distance.

Chapter Fourteen

A horse pawed the earth, and, moaning, I opened my eyes, praying this had been a dream, that I'd wake up in camp and hear old Chuck snorting, impatient to be grained. Didn't happen, though.

It took a while to focus, but, when the blurs cleared, I found Kim Harrigan staring down at me. He stood holding the reins to his horse, relief washing across his face upon the realization that I hadn't broken my neck. Quickly he ground-reined his mount and, joints popping, dropped beside me.

"Don't move," he ordered when I bent my knees.

Recalling the captain's instructions, I shook my head. "No. First thing you do when you get bucked off is you get right back on." That's what I had done back at headquarters the morning Chuck left me tasting gravel. Difference was, back then, the only thing I'd hurt was my pride.

Kim stopped me as I stirred, his grip strong against my right shoulder. "No. First thing you do is make sure you ain't bad hurt."

"I'm not hurt," I argued, forcing myself up until the searing pain caused me to scream, and I collapsed, tears flowing down dirty cheeks. It felt as if someone had chopped off my left arm with a saber.

I've lost count of the times I've told some green-horn my philosophy about horses. Probably told a score of you-all it a time or two. If you've never been hurt, you've never been horseback. Well, I've been hurt more times than I'd care to recall, but that wreck near Deadman Cañon was the first bad one, the one I remember most.

"Arm's busted." That was Kim's diagnosis, which you didn't have to be an old pill-roller to figure out. "Anything else hurtin'? Your insides feel all right?"

At first, only my head hurt, but the agony in my arm diminished any other smarting. Grinding my teeth against the pain, I shook my head again. Through tear-filled eyes, I saw him frown and back away from me, moving to his horse, pulling the rifle out of the scabbard. Only then did I hear the clopping hoofs.

Kim didn't even twitch, just stared. Somewhere behind me, saddle leather squeaked, and spurs sang out a melody.

"For all I know," Kim addressed the newcomer, "you was with them two." He kept the rifle at his waist, though, never aiming it.

A second or two later, Mary Holliday knelt beside me. Her hands reached out as she smiled, this angel, but when she took my arm in her hands, I yelped in pain, my illusion gone. Angel? More like a witch.

"Arm's busted," she said.

I snapped back with a curse, a good one, too, for a busted-up fourteen-year-old.

"You got a temper on you, Hart." Before Kim or I knew what she was doing, she shoved her boot against my armpit and gave my arm a wicked jerk.

Yelling, crying, cursing even louder, I rocked and roared until it hit me that the arm didn't hurt so much.

"I set it, but we need something for a splint." She spoke over her shoulder to Kim, who wandered away, rifle in tow, and returned a few minutes later with the skeletal remains of a cholla. They helped me sit up, and Kim ripped up his bandanna to fasten the makeshift splint. Mary untied her neckerchief, too, which became my sling.

"He ought to see a doctor," Mary told Kim. "Make sure his insides ain't busted up and bleeding. I'll ride with you if you like."

"Nearest one's in White Oaks," he said.

"What about Roswell?"

Kim's head shook. "Dead. Got struck by lightnin'. I was there a month ago when they was buryin' the ol' sawbones."

"Ain't that fitting."

"I'll get him to the ranch," Kim said. "Maybe we can catch his horse. If not Caleb's horse, then the horse of that *hombre* I shot."

That's when it dawned on me that Kim Harrigan had been shooting from the hills. He had knocked Earl Sutton out of the saddle, had saved my life. I don't know what I had been thinking when the shooting started, maybe that it was Mary Holliday rescuing me, perhaps nothing seeing how fast things had happened.

"That *hombre* was Earl Sutton," I said. "Other one was Tim."

Kim stared blankly before shooting Mary a

glance—I reckon to check her reaction to the names—but Mary could play poker. If the names meant anything to her, you couldn't read it on her face.

"The Suttons." Kim shook his head and spit. He couldn't have made out their faces from the hills, just their actions. After another sigh, he muttered an oath. "Well," Kim continued, "anyway, Hobbs Wallace has set a few bones in his days. And the capt'n can fetch a doctor."

"Then I ain't riding with you," Mary said. "Not that way."

"I didn't invite you." He scowled at her, and we both stared at him as he explained again. "Like I said, for all I know, you was part of that gang. They might have killed the boy."

"I wasn't with those two, mister." Mary had a pretty mean scowl herself. "I don't murder boys, even if they be Harts."

"I spotted sign. Three men were in that hide-out, alterin' brands," Kim said, unconvinced.

"In case you ain't noticed, I ain't a man."

"You're a rustler."

"Like I told Caleb, I only take what's owed me." She was spitting out the words again, angry, almost shaking with rage. "How much you think a life's worth? A dozen head? Two dozen? A hundred? How about the life of my husband?"

Well, they just stared at one another, glaring, snarling, forgetting all about me and my broken arm. Had to clear my throat—twice—before they looked back at me.

"She's telling the truth," I told Kim. "While I was chasing Tim Sutton, I spied another rider." I explained how I had seen a man on a paint horse,

THE HART BRAND

143

the one who had ridden to the ridge line and spurred away after seeing what was going on. The way it struck me, he had to be the third rustler. Most likely he had been checking the back door, so to speak, making sure the Suttons weren't being followed.

"Paint horse?" Kim asked.

"Yes, sir."

He spit out tobacco juice and returned the Brown-Merrill into the saddle scabbard. "Paint horse," he repeated, this time with disgust. At first, I thought he was just acting like a cowboy. You-all know what I mean. Cowboys got little use for a paint horse. Remember the joke? Why did Indian chiefs send their warriors to battle on paint horses? To make 'em mad. Only then Kim muttered a name underneath his breath. Cannon Defroy. It meant nothing to me, but in time I would learn that Cannon Defroy's name was on Slim Reed's list of suspected rustlers. Everybody in the Tularosa Basin knew Defroy rode a piebald mare.

Determining it too late to start for the ranch, we made camp back at Deadman Cañon. Mary Holliday tried to run down my horse, but it had too much of a headstart. Kim said Chuck would likely make a beeline back home, so they gave me a boost into Kim's saddle, and we took it easy returning to the hide-out. Earl Sutton was gone, too, having left a trail of blood. During the ruction, with me chasing Tim Sutton and Kim Harrigan shooting from the hills, he must have pulled himself into his saddle and took off south. Had it not been for me, Kim probably would have gone after him, though he told me it didn't matter

much. The Sutton brothers were finished in this
territory, or so we thought.

As Mary fried salt pork and boiled coffee, Kim
cleaned his rifle and filled me in. He had sent me
out hunting rabbits to get me away from the hide-
out. Gut feeling told him the rustlers would return that day or the next. If they hadn't appeared
that day, he would have sent me off somewhere
else the next. And the next.

"Figured to keep you away from any stray bullet," he said. "Didn't work out that way."

"Well, I didn't get shot," I said, then wished I
had. A bullet scar. By grab, that would have been
something. I mean, if they had winged me in the
arm or leg or something along those lines. . . . A
bullet in my head—that I wouldn't have cared
much for. The vision returned of Earl Sutton
drawing that Remington revolver.

"He was going to kill me!" I shouted.

"Maybe not." Kim shook his head, although
he had voiced a similar opinion to Mary during
their earlier confrontation. "Might have planned
on takin' you back here a prisoner, you see, then
tyin' you up, leavin' you so they could get away."

From the cook fire, Mary sniggered. "Then he
might have starved to death, fed the coyotes and
turkey vultures. Bullet would have been quicker.
It's murder just the same."

"Maybe so." Kim spit. He fished out his tobacco
and knife, and shook his head. "When I saw that
rider . . . didn't know it was the Suttons . . . pull
his pistol, I had to shoot. Maybe he wasn't gonna
do you no harm, but couldn't chance it, though I
had to risk a shot over your head to hit him."

"Maybe . . ."—Mary spoke with a great deal of

sarcasm—"maybe he spied a rattler and you shot an innocent man."

That left Kim speechless for a moment. Reckon that thought had never occurred to him, but I broke the silence and told Kim he had done right. They were rustlers, bound for Dead-man Cañon, and I won't forget that look Earl Sutton gave me. Jim Gilliland and Slim Reed had the same hatred in their eyes. For that matter, so did Mary Holliday, sometimes.

"Didn't mean to get you hurt, Caleb," Kim said. "Figured you'd be out of harm's way. Not sure how the capt'n'll take this."

Mary mumbled something, but I couldn't make out the words over the spitting grease from the frying pan.

"It's not your fault," I told Kim. "Nobody's fault but the Sutton brothers."

"I had a good spot in the hills," Kim said. "When I watched you ride up and join the Suttons, I didn't know what to do. Then, when I saw Earl draw his pistol, I had to fire. Hoped I wouldn't hit you by mistake." He had said as much already, but I guess he was still trying to convince himself that he had done the right thing. Guilt was written all over his face, and I figured Kim Harrigan was not a man who liked violence, unlike Slim Reed. Kim detested it, hated what he was doing for the captain, but—the words rang out in my head once more: *You ride for the brand.*

Suddenly Kim laughed. "Tell you the truth, Caleb, I couldn't believe my eyes when I saw you take off after Tim. That scene was like one of them woodcut engravin's on a dime novel cover. What was you thinkin'?"

"I wasn't. Just mad is all. Mad and scared."

"Well. . . ." His smile widened. "You're a hero, Caleb. How does that feel?"

Mary had turned from the fire to stare at me, too, and I tried to shake my head, dismiss Kim's idea as pure foolishness. I wound up saying that I wasn't any hero, was just doing my job. I could see Mary roll her eyes before spitting out snuff and returning her attention to the salt pork.

After supper, the arm started hurting again, so Mary made me take a little swallow from a bottle of hers labeled **Tincture of Arnica.** Kim had a bottle in his saddlebags, and he sweetened my coffee with Booth & Co. Superior Dry Gin. Between the medicines, my newfound status as a bona-fide hero, and Mary's dancing eyes, I soon forgot all about my broken arm as the pain numbed, and I drifted off to sleep.

When I awoke the next morning, Kim had already saddled his horse, and Mary Holliday was gone.

With Kim leading me on his horse, it took two days before we reached Hart headquarters. Poor Kim. Can't tell you how sorry I felt for him. High-heeled boots aren't meant for walking, cowboys hate to be afoot, and Kim was limping those last few miles. He had worn holes in boots and socks, and his feet got blistered something fierce. Stubborn as I was becoming, I made him let me walk some, too, but, even when I walked, he just led his cow pony along, wouldn't ride at all.

It had warmed up that week, and twice we saw rattlesnakes. The first time I sat in the saddle, watching with amazement as Kim grabbed his lariat, uncoiled it, and walked to the snake. You shot snakes with your pistols or rifles, or so I had thought, only to learn that's not the cowboy way. Kim lashed out with the end of his lariat, the rope whirling, popping like gunshots as he whipped the rattler to death.

Once he had finished, he pulled out his knife, cut off the rattles—that was only a small one; the second one he killed had ten rattles—and grinned while walking back, rolling up the hemp rope.

"What's the matter?" he asked.

Reckon my jaw about touched the saddle horn. My reply came out in a stutter, and he chuckled as he returned the lariat.

"Knowed quite a few hands who could do that a-horseback," he said. "Used to do it that way myself till I seen Jim McPherson flip up a rattler right into his own face. Scared Jim out of twenty-five years. Scared his horse all the way to San ngelo. Probably scared the snake out of Texas. After that, I figured killin' snakes was one thing a cowhand should do afoot." He handed me the rattles.

Though I kept looking for Mary, we didn't see anyone until we walked down the hill to the ranch, dogs growling and barking as if they hadn't seen us before, and Hobbs Wallace come limping out from the privy, as fast as his bad leg would let him move.

"Caleb. . . ." He smiled with great relief. "We about give you up for dead."

Leading us inside the bunkhouse, he explained how Chuck had come galloping up a few days back. The captain looked worried sick, Hobbs said, and rode out with Jesús Salazar and Rex

Steele to find us. They had taken old Chuck along, hoping I'd be able to ride him and not be tied over the saddle.

Hobbs fed us biscuits and beans while he checked my arm, commending Kim for his doctoring. Wanting to give Mary credit, I started to brag that Kim had had some help, but a sharp stare and grunt from Kim told me to leave well enough alone. He was right. I didn't know what Hobbs Wallace thought or knew about Mary Magdalene Holliday, but I sure understood the depth of her hatred for anything Hart except, I hoped, me.

Over my protests, they put me to bed, saying I needed rest, and I guess I did because I slept the rest of the day, didn't even budge when the boys came in from the roundup, or when the captain returned late that evening with Salazar and Rex.

In fact, when I finally woke to the smell of coffee and bacon, the captain had already ridden off, and even Dickie Fergusson had crawled from underneath his blankets and was sipping coffee. There was another association meeting, Kim informed me, this one in White Oaks. Captain Hart would bring the doctor back when he returned.

Once I got my boots back on and made my way to the table, the boys started applauding and cheering, hailing me as the hero who had shot it out with the Daltons and the Youngers and Billy the Kid and Jessie Evans.

I let them have their fun. Actually it made me proud, almost as if I were a hero. Rex told me I had given everyone quite a scare. They weren't much good at reading sign, and the first tracks they had found revealed one man in boots leading a horse carrying some weight. To them, it read that Kim Harrigan was bringing my body home. It's a shame they didn't find my boot prints. They didn't even see the cañon hide-out, only dried blood (Earl Sutton's, though they had no way of knowing that). If they had followed the trail a little more, or had a one of them been half the tracker Kim Harrigan was, they could have learned the truth. But they were cowboys, not government scouts.

"Too bad we didn't run across each other," I said.

"Big country," Rex explained.

"Did you find the cattle the Suttons were trying to steal?"

His head shook—they weren't looking for cattle, just me, dead or alive—and suddenly that big Rex Steele grin parted the wrinkles in Rex's face. "Frank looked right relieved when we got home," he said. "Took a weight off his shoulders, certain-sure. Yes, sir, he was right joyful that he didn't have to go out and buy you a coffin. You know how tight he is with a greenback."

After breakfast, we went outside to mount—Dickie Fergusson last as always—and I talked things over with Rex.

Roundup had started, so I'd have chores to do, one-armed or not. Couldn't do much on horse-back, with my arm splinted and in a sling, but I could help Hobbs Wallace prepare grub and ride out in the chuck wagon. That sounded fine to me.

"That's why Frank pays me a foreman's wage," Rex said.

Most of the boys were ready to go, waiting on

Dickie Fergusson to throw his saddle on his mount's back. I looked around the corrals, glad to be back . . . home, it struck me. Home.

"Where's Chuck?" I asked.

Well, Rex, he wasn't smiling any more, and he shuffled his feet in the dust and, rare for him, struggled to find the words.

"Well, Caleb, it's . . . well, it's like I was telling you in the bunkhouse." He kept staring at the dirt clods, Rex typically being a man to look you in the eye. "The captain figured Chuck, temperamental as he could be, had bucked you off something bad. I don't know. He figured Chuck had killed you."

Rex didn't say it, and this is just something I came to believe over the next month, but Captain Hart had never been one to jump to conclusions, go off, like the saying goes, half-cocked. That had been Tim Sutton. But the captain was drinking now, pretty hard, dulling his senses, or maybe drinking to forget. It was the whiskey, I think, that caused it.

"Where's Chuck?" I repeated, agitated now.

Rex took in a deep breath and slowly exhaled. "Frank killed him."

Chapter Fifteen

Those next few weeks contain some of my favorite memories as winter passed and spring, though wet and dreary, settled over southern New Mexico. Captain Hart returned home a few days later, doctor in tow, and the sawbones commended Kim Harrigan on a fine job of setting my broken arm (not knowing Mary Holliday had done it). The old doc removed my cholla splint and put on a hard plaster cast, though I retained Mary's silk bandanna for my sling. Later, that arm would itch something awful, but I soon grew used to being a one-armed cowboy.

I'd help Hobbs Wallace with the cooking, and, when branding started, I went around with an empty flour sack, holding it open as Jesús Salazar and Manuel used their pocket knives to castrate calves and toss the—well, you-all know what I mean—into the sack. First time, Jesús grinned at me and, seeing how my Spanish wasn't good, spoke in broken English.

"Prairie oysters . . . you . . . like?"

I made a face.

"Best eating . . ."—he rubbed his stomach—"in world."

"I'll take your word for it," I told him.

At supper, though, turned out old Jesús Salazar

was right. Hobbs Wallace knew how to bread those oysters and fry them till they were just downright delectable. Then again, Hobbs Wallace could doctor up an air-tight of tomatoes till you'd think you were eating in one of Denver's best restaurants.

Another time, Rex Steele hollered at me to come over and help as he dragged a soon to be Hart steer to the branding fire. Jesús Salazar pinned down the animal, Manuel went to work with his knife, and Dickie Fergusson pulled out a branding iron and held it toward me. Iron was heavy, and Dickie had to help me guide it, me having only one good arm, but I pushed the heart outline onto the reddish hide. Fire and smoke shot out, and that calf let out a howl.

"Keep it there," Dickie told me. "Little bit longer."

The smell took some getting used to, but when Dickie nodded, we pulled away the iron, and let the steer run back to its mama. I saw the Hart brand, my handiwork, and Dickie said: "That'll keep."

The captain proved himself to be one of the best ropers on the range, too. I marveled at how he could throw a loop, even heard him laugh a time or two. Good times they were. Hard work. Dirty and smelly, especially in water-logged weather, but I wouldn't trade those memories for all the beef in this country.

Yep, mighty fine times.

Most days we spent in our makeshift camp, returning to the ranch only when Hobbs Wallace needed supplies. There must have been dozens of branding camps scattered across the basin.

Cowhands from several ranches pushed beef down the Capitans and other mountains to the summer pastures, and Kim Harrigan rode out somewhere, alone, doing his thankless job of searching for rustlers. I can't say we forgot about the Fountains, about the Suttons, about Slim Reed or Cannon Defroy, about Oliver Lee and James Gilliland, but we pushed those thoughts—especially concerning the Fountains—aside. Too much work to do, and I was learning how to cowboy.

'Course, Fred Hutchins reminded us of those unsettling things when he drove his Michigan surrey to camp shortly before supper one evening in April. His face looked more windburned than normal, and he climbed down from the wagon, huffing and puffing as he tugged at the front of his coat and stormed to the campfire.

" 'Evening, Mister Hutchins!" Dickie Fergusson called out. "Pour you some Arbuckle's?"

Mr. Hutchins didn't answer, didn't speak until his eyes lighted on Captain Hart over by the Studebaker chuck wagon where the captain was formulating plans for the morrow with Hobbs Wallace.

"Branding a lot more beef of yours, Frank, than I am H-Bar cattle down by Walnut Draw," he said, a challenge in his voice. The Hutchins brothers were in charge of the roundup crews working that area, just north of Old George's line shack.

"I run more beef down there." The captain walked toward the fire and filled two mugs of stout brew. "So does the Rocking R." He handed one cup toward our guest, and reluctantly Mr. Hutchins took it.

"Maybe so, Frank, but the Rocking R and me had an agreement to let me graze, and I'm losing a lot of beef."

"My man's working on it."

"He ain't doing the job!" The words came from the angry rancher's mouth like a gunshot. "The deal we made, Frank, and only because you insisted on it, was Slim Reed would control things east and south of your kingdom." I couldn't help but notice the way he said kingdom, like he was belittling the captain, and Mr. Hutchins a guest in our camp! This wasn't like Fred Hutchins at all. "Your man Harrigan would clean up things here."

"On my range." Captain Hart emptied his coffee, untouched, and slung the cup toward the wreck pan.

"But it ain't just your range, Frank. It's Rocking R land, it's the Flying K, L-Over-S, and Double Diamond. And it's the Bar-H. And I'm sick of having beef stole from me."

"Harrigan ran off the Sutton brothers." The captain put his hands on his hips. "Shot one of them. And he doesn't get paid the bounty the association pays Slim Reed."

"He didn't run nobody off," Mr. Hutchins said. "Slim Reed found Sutton, the big one, the one your man shot. Slim tracked him down in Eddy. Shot him dead. His brother and that no-account with the paint horse, they got away, but Slim'll bring them to justice, too." He looked down at me. "You don't have to worry about Earl Sutton no more, bub. He's dead. Slim Reed took care of him." He nodded curtly. "That should make you feel better, feel proud. We avenged you, the

Southeastern New Mexico Stock Growers' Association did."

Well, it didn't make me feel proud or better. Made me sick.

"Turns out," Mr. Hutchins said, addressing Captain Hart again, "Sutton spent time in the Colorado penitentiary. Two years. For rustling. You should have knowed that, Frank. You should have."

"I knew it."

Fred Hutchins looked as if he had been gut-shot. "You knowed it? And you hired that . . . ?"

"I don't care what a man's done in his past, Fred. I gave him a chance. Turned out I was wrong, but I wouldn't do nothing different. The Suttons worked hard before they turned bad on me."

"Turned bad . . . that's one way of putting it. Turned bad like that Holliday boy and. . . ."

I never even saw Captain Hart throw the punch, only heard the *crunch*, and, before I knew it, Fred Hutchins lay sprawling in the mud and muck, and the captain was circling the fire, ready to pound the man even more. Rex jumped to his feet, but it took him and Hobbs Wallace to pull the captain back. The rest of us scattered from the fire, unsure, uncertain, and Mr. Hutchins was sitting up, testing his jaw, spitting out blood and saliva, his lips busted good.

"You had no call to do that," he said on his haunches. "You got no right. . . ."

"You got no right!" the captain bellowed. "You come into my camp like this. You got a problem with me or my methods, you take them up with me, you don't question me in front of my men and you don't. . . ." He let the rest go unfinished.

Dickie Fergusson and I helped Mr. Hutchins to his feet, and Rex and Hobbs Wallace turned the captain loose. It started misting rain.

"Now I want you two boys to shake hands," Hobbs Wallace instructed. "Go on now. This may be your ranch, Captain, and it may be your cattle getting stole, Fred, but this is my camp, and I don't allow no fisticuffs. Go on, I said, shake."

Turning his head aside, Mr. Hutchins spit out more blood. "You should remember Ab Northrup," he mumbled.

"I said shake hands, Fred, or skedaddle!"

Unsmiling, they shook. Afterward, Hobbs Wallace gave Mr. Hutchins a rag to stanch the bleeding, then refilled his cup. Not much was said—by grab, nobody talked—until Mr. Hutchins rose.

"I said what I come here to say," he announced. "Maybe we should call another meeting, get things cleared up." He let out a sigh, shaking his head, and, when he spoke again, the bitterness had left his voice. "The ranch is all Judge and I got, Frank. We're gonna stop them thieves from driving us to ruin, with or without you. That's all I got to say, Frank. That's all I come to say."

He strode back to his surrey, swallowed up by the mist and darkening skies, a proud man, like the captain, strong, robust, and a man, much like my father, on the verge of financial ruin. That was the last time I saw Fred Hutchins—alive I mean. Next time I saw him—well . . . I'll get to that directly.

Untypical for New Mexico, the rains set in, only not hard, just numbing cold, sprinkles here and there. Rex Steele kept wishing there would come a gully-washer, just to get it over with, but God didn't listen. Every once in a while, we'd think the rains, the fogs, the clouds and gloom would move on, and things would clear up, but that never lasted. A couple of our crew came down with colds, and most nights we spent around campfires trying to dry our clothes, or, at least, our socks.

"How'd you sleep?" I remember asking Dickie Fergusson one particularly miserable morning.

"Fine," he snapped. "I love sleeping with rain water in my face."

As I tossed fuel onto the campfire, although I figured I'd never get really warm again, the captain squatted by me.

"Your arm up for a chore?" he asked.

"Sure."

"Think you can saddle a horse with your right arm?"

"If I'm in no hurry." My joke must have failed, because the captain didn't appear amused. "I can do it. I've been practicing."

"I'm gonna draw you a map to Roswell. You'll ride Penny. She ain't as ornery as. . . ." He couldn't say Chuck's name. "She ain't too tall, and I got you a Morgan saddle. Don't weigh more'n a dozen pounds, and Penny's as gentle a horse as I got. With your right arm, I'm betting you can handle this deal. Leave the bridle on. Don't think you can manage that with one good hand, and just loosen the cinch at night. Don't take the saddle off unless you have to. Likely you can saddle Penny with one arm, but the bridle and bit would be tougher. And don't go near any cactus. Cactus scares her. She jumps over it . . . I mean jumps . . . so give any cholla or yucca a wide berth. My guess is a lightning strike knocked her into a bed of cactus a couple years back. Anyway, I want you to fetch Harrigan, bring him back to the ranch. The association is going to meet again in Lincoln next week. I want Harrigan with me."

"Yes, sir."

"You'll ride out after breakfast."

"Yes, sir." I didn't want to leave the warmth of the fire, but made myself rise. "Best give Penny her breakfast, too."

"Caleb."

Our eyes met, only briefly, then he tilted his head, motioning me to sit back down, and began stuffing his pipe with tobacco. Frank Hart never was one for telling stories—except during our ride to El Paso that one time—or giving advice, but once I sat beside him, he began talking, not that much, not even looking at me.

"Don't feel sorry for what happened to Earl Sutton."

"No, sir."

"Ain't your fault."

"Yes, sir. I know that."

"We do what we think is right, Caleb. That's one thing my pa, your grandfather, practically beat into Lucas and me. You always side with what's right. Not what the law says is right, not even always what the Good Book says is right. Not what anybody else says, but by what your gut tells you is right. Be your own man. That's what my daddy done. That's what I've done here . . . it's why I ain't ashamed for what happened to Ab Northrup or . . . or Holliday. It's what I'll always do, and that's what Lucas and me, that's what we expect from you."

He placed the pipe down on a rock, and reached inside his Mackinaw. I thought he was looking for a match, but he withdrew a pewter flask instead. Staring at the fire, rain water dripping off the brim of his hat, he unscrewed the top and brought the whiskey to his lips.

Dickie had left the fire to see to his horse, and I decided to do the same. I don't think Captain Hart even knew I had left.

Well, I reached Roswell with no trouble and, following the captain's instructions, waited for Kim Harrigan at the livery. The next day, he rode in, surprised to see me, but glad—until I told him about the Southeastern New Mexico Stock Growers' Association meeting in Lincoln, and what had happened to Earl Sutton.

Kim swore. What bothered me was that Slim Reed would collect the $100 bonus for killing Earl Sutton, and maybe more for running Tim Sutton and Cannon Defroy out of the territory, if they had left. That's not what troubled Kim, though.

We grabbed a bite to eat at some adobe *cantina*, then made our way for the ranch, passing near Deadman Cañon without a word. When we reached the ranch, it was deserted, except for barking dogs and squawking chickens, so we fed and watered our horses and went inside the bunkhouse.

I used a piece of baling wire to scratch my itching arm inside the cast, while Kim rustled up supper: crackers and an air-tight of peaches.

"Slim Reed gonna be at that meetin'?" he asked.

"I expect," I answered, though I had no way of knowing.

I did tell him about the little row at camp between Fred Hutchins and the captain. He didn't have much of a reaction. I wanted to talk about Mary Holliday, but instead I asked about Thaddeus Hall.

"Told you before . . . I didn't know him."

"But you knew Ab Northrup."

He forked in a mouthful of peach.

Well, I had to ask, had to know once and for all. I didn't think anyone else would tell me the truth, except Kim Harrigan.

"Did . . . did Captain Hart kill Ab Northrup, too?"

Chapter Sixteen

"No." I'll never forget the way Kim said it, the way he just kept staring ahead, only not really seeing anything, or the sound of his voice—like a dead man talking. I guess I already knew what he'd say next, but the words still made me shiver.

"I did."

He dropped his fork in the air-tight, and slid the tin can across the table. Only then did he look me in the eye.

"He was eatin' breakfast when I shot him." A mirthless noise, more sigh than laugh, escaped Kim's throat, and he shook his head. "Just squattin' by the fire, sloppin' up beans with a tortilla."

Well, I knew a little about the story, from what others, including the captain, had told me. One of many Texians who fled to New Mexico Territory, most likely to escape the arm of the law, Ab Northrup found an outlaw haven from Seven Rivers to Silver City. He homesteaded a little spread, but mostly Ab Northrup rustled cattle and stole horses. Some say he even hunted Apache scalps, but that sounds mighty far-fetched. County solicitors never did a thing to punish Northrup, though he had been jailed a time or two, including the time in 1886 when Captain Hart swore out a complaint and had him arrested. Once Northrup got acquitted, he slapped a Hart brand on one of his own beeves, then accused the captain of rustling. He filed a suit, though I don't think it ever went to court, wrote letters that would be called libel in this day and age, and went right on stealing and lying. "He was a burr under the capt'n's saddle blanket," Kim Harrigan said. "We were all sick of him."

On March 10, 1887, Kim Harrigan came across Northrup's camp down around the Peñasco River. Northrup was alone. No incriminating evidence, not even any cattle or horses nearby, except Northrup's own blue roan. Just squatting beside the fire, plate in his lap, fork in his hand, and a handkerchief tucked in the front of his shirt like a napkin. A man minding his own business.

"Just struck me that here was a fellow causin' a peck of trouble," Kim said. "Law wouldn't do nothin', so I did. I just pulled my rifle out, worked the bolt, and took aim." His head dropped.

"Did . . . did my uncle . . . did Captain Hart hire . . . er . . . ask you to . . . to kill him?"

"Nah. No bounty on Northrup's head, and the association hadn't been formed yet. No, I was just ridin' for the brand and, in my young mind, seemed the right thing to do. That's what the capt'n always told us boys . . . Rex, Old George, Salazar . . . durin' the nigh three years I rode for the brand. Do what you think's right. So, it appeared to me that killin' Northrup was right. I shot him in the head. Can't say I was aimin' for his head or his heart. I don't even remember pullin' the trigger. Then I rode down to camp, put out his fire, turned his horse loose, and slipped the bullet casin' under Northrup's head. A warnin', you see. Let other rustlers know things was changin'."

"What happened?" I asked.

"Nothin'. The capt'n took the blame from the pettifoggin' lawyers, and some newspapers, but there was never any writs served. Not again' the capt'n. Not again' me. I told the capt'n what I done, and he just nodded. Three, four months later I come across another rustler, and I killed him, too, though he at least seen me, even sent lead my way. I left him sprawlin' in the sand, put another shell under his head. Another warnin'."

Which didn't strike me as real smart. Leaving a Winchester shell under a dead man's head was one thing, but there weren't a whole lot of .58-caliber Brown-Merrills in the territory. Maybe Kim wanted to build up a reputation as a gunman back then. I don't know. He didn't say. It also struck me that, once Kim Harrigan became known as a man-killer, any fool could shoot someone, slide an empty brass casing under the dead man's head, and holler out "Kim Harrigan done it!" Mind you, I didn't say anything. I just listened to Kim's . . . reckon you'd call it his confession.

"Pretty soon after that, rustlin' got scarce, though I warrant the drought that come up on us a year or so later had more to do with that," he said. "Anyhow, Caleb, after that second killin', lots of folks got more than a bit uncomfortable. Businessmen was pushin' for statehood, didn't think havin' some thirty-a-month cowhand gunnin' down rustlers was an image New Mexico needed." He let out another humorless laugh.

"Seems they've forgotten all about that . . . what, nine years later . . . hirin' Slim Reed and all. Well, Capt'n Hart figured it might be good if I left the territory. He wrote a letter to some associates of his in Wyoming, and I went north to Cheyenne. Became what they called a stock detective. Sounds mighty fancy, but what they wanted wasn't Kim Harrigan but Slim Reed. 'Course, that's what I'd become.

"I killed two men in New Mexico. Ain't a day gone by that I ain't regretted it. Honest to God, Caleb, if I could trade places with Ab Northrup today, I surely would. Killin' eats at a body. But I didn't kill nobody in Wyoming. That didn't make the men at the Wyoming Stock Growers' Association happy. I run off some boys, then one day in 'Eighty-Eight the ranchers formed a vigilance committee, and we paid this gal a visit. She . . . well . . . they called her Cattle Kate, and she had started what you might call a bawdy house in Sweetwater. She'd take beef on the hoof as payment. We rode there, and them ranchers put a noose over her head. Hung her partner, Jim Averill, too. Turns out, though, that some of them cattlemen had called on Kate before, called on her social, sort of. And they hanged her, anyway. Well, hangin' a woman, that was nothin' I wanted any part of. And I told them men. . . ." He spit. "Men? Gutless cowards they was. But I wasn't no better. I let 'em hang Kate and Averill. Reckon I was as much a coward as they was. But I told 'em what I thought, quit 'em, got a job punchin' cattle south of Laramie. Figured I'd come back to the Hart someday.

"They hired themselves a new stock detective, and pret' soon rustlers was turnin' up with shells underneath their dead heads. Reckon I started somethin'. Well, I just worked cattle, then one day I find myself starin' at two deputy sheriffs and about a dozen boys who rode for various ranches belongin' to the Wyoming Stock Growers' Association. They tossed a runnin' iron at my feet, said I'd been rustlin'. I called every mother's son of 'em a liar, and we had ourselves a pretty good fist fight." He laughed again. "I lost. Took me to jail, and, before I knowed it, I was doin' five years at The Big House. The cattle barons . . . they was behind it, gettin' even with me, I guess, learnin' me a lesson."

"But you were innocent!"

"Was I?" Kim shook his head. "That ain't how I looked at it, Caleb. Maybe I hadn't done no rustlin', but I sure felt guilty. And five years in prison ain't nothin' considerin' them two men I killed down here. Or they could have killed me, left a casin' under my head, but I guess, maybe, they feared what Capt'n Hart would say or do if I turned up dead like that. Soon as I got out, I taken a job swampin' a saloon in Cheyenne . . . only job I could find . . . then the capt'n's telegraph reached me. Offerin' me a job. So I come south. Reckon I knowed what would happen, but I come anyway, and now, well, it's happenin'."

"Why don't you quit?" I suggested. "Go back to Texas? Get a fresh start somewhere else? California maybe?"

"I've studied on it. Studied hard. But I'm hopin' I can make things right, and I sure owe the capt'n. All I want to do is show these ranchers that there ain't got to be killin'. That the way Slim Reed, the way we've done things, that's all changin'. It's. . . ."

Slowly he rose, muttering that he'd best check on the horses. I knew the silence had returned, the brooding. I was to blame for it, too, by bringing up Ab Northrup.

Captain Hart showed up that evening, and the next morning they rode off to Lincoln. Weeks would pass before I'd see Kim Harrigan again.

Kim made his point, though. I don't want you-all to think Slim Reed was doing all the business with rustlers. Reed had killed two men, but Kim rounded up a few rustlers, and he didn't shoot them down, either. Two Mexicans he took to the jail in Roswell. Another he handed over to what law there was in White Oaks. Others he drove into the Sacramentos or across the border. They say—and I'm not sure if it's a big windy or the truth—that he even caught a man rustling from Oliver Lee, and turned that fellow over to Pat Garrett in Las Cruces.

Meanwhile, with most of the branding done, we were back at the bunkhouse. That's when Rex Steele gave me the idea. I had that piece of baling wire, scratching inside my cast, when he shook his head and told me I'd best be careful. "You cut yourself with that wire, and that arm mortifies, then Hobbs will have to saw it off, and Frank won't like it one bit."

Well, I right carefully pulled the wire from the underside of the plaster, and got to staring at it.

Next morning, I finished my breakfast in no

time, and, as the boys filed out of the bunkhouse, I told Hobbs Wallace that the captain wanted to see him. Grumbling, Hobbs wiped his hands on a dirty rag, tossed it on the table, and complained as Dickie Fergusson slurped his coffee while cracking his toes in front of the stove.

I couldn't have planned things any better, because Captain Hart had come from his house, and was saddling his horse in front of the corral. As Hobbs Wallace started to ask the captain what he wanted, I told Hobbs just to turn around.

"What is this?" he said with a sneer.

"Just watch," I said, lugging my Morgan saddle, blanket, and bridle to Penny.

"Boy, I ain't got no time for your foolishness." He whirled on his good leg and voiced his complaints with Captain Hart, who tightened the cinch while shooting me a curious look.

"Figured you wouldn't want to miss this, Hobbs." I tossed the blanket over Penny's back, then the saddle.

By now, everyone looked a mite bewildered. As I awkwardly worked the latigo with my one hand, my eyes brightened in self-amusement, and I asked: "Where's Dickie?"

Leaning against the corral fence, the captain had fished out his pipe and began stuffing tobacco. Rex, Salazar, Hobbs, and the rest of the boys stared at the bunkhouse. Rex started grinning, and then he shouted: "Fergusson, you sorry cuss! I ain't burning daylight waiting on you no more! Get out here, now, or draw your time!"

Well, the bunkhouse door flew open, and Dickie Fergusson charged into the dawn, trying to finish his coffee before giving up and tossing it near the barn. For a moment, I got really nervous. What if this doesn't work? What if Dickie gets bad hurt? Briefly I thought about shouting out a warning, but by then Dickie disappeared inside the tack shed. Seconds later, he raced outside, lugging his saddle, staring ahead at us, determination in his face.

And next . . . the baling wire pulled tight, and we weren't looking at Dickie's face any more but the soles of his boots. When he landed on his backside, splattering mud, everyone broke out hooting and hollering. Even Captain Hart doubled over in laughter.

You see, I had clipped off a good piece of wire in the barn, securing one end on the underside of Dickie's saddle, hoping he wouldn't notice, rushed as he was prone to be every morning and dark as the shed was. The other end I tied to the bottom of the post where his saddle sat.

Dickie sat up, shaking his head, cussing Rex Steele for playing such a joke. He was kicking mad as he tried to jerk the saddle off the ground, only to have the wire pull it back into the mud again. We laughed harder, Hobbs Wallace the hardest of all now, and then Dickie noticed the wire, saw its trail to the shed, and he cussed some more.

"Rex!" he bellowed.

"Ain't my doing!" Rex shouted back. "But I sure wish it had been!"

"We're waiting on you, Fergusson," Captain Hart said as he finished his smoke. Gathering his reins, he turned to me. "Was I you," he said, "I'd be right careful when mounting your horse, especially after your arm heals. Right stirrup tucked under the saddle. Burrs under the saddle blanket.

Loosened cinch. Maybe even a snake in your soogans, or a scorpion in your boot."

"I'll remember that," I said.

Dickie had stopped cussing, and started fumbling with the wire, as saddle leather squeaked and we got ready to ride. Still chuckling, Hobbs Wallace limped past Dickie on the way back inside, and Rex, Salazar, and everyone gave me a pat on the shoulder.

"Him?" Dickie couldn't believe it. "The kid? It was Caleb?" His answer came in various chuckles and guffaws.

"You're a dead man, Caleb!" Dickie fired out, but with humor now. Most good cowboys can take a joke played on them because they know they'll get revenge sometime down the road.

I mention this story for a couple of reasons. One is that was maybe the first time I really felt part of the Hart Ranch. Sure, I had traded shots with Tim Sutton, I had heard stories, true stories, personal stories, from both Captain Hart and Kim Harrigan, and I had already made lasting friendships. I'd branded cattle, strung wire, earned my keep, but I'll never forget the looks everyone gave me that morning. All I had done was play a practical joke on the always-late Dickie Fergusson, yet humor's a key element of life on a cattle ranch, and I had made my mark. I had found a place. The Hart Ranch had become home.

The second reason is because of that humor. The way I remember things, that was the last time anyone on the Hart range laughed that spring.

Two days later, I think it was, Rex Steele and I were graining the horses in the corral when the dogs started barking. When we looked up, we spied the Hutchins brothers' Michigan surrey topping the hill, a saddled bay horse in tow.

"That ain't . . . ," Rex started, then tossed the pitchfork aside. He ducked underneath the top rail, and stepped out of the corral. I followed him.

"That's Old George," Rex said. It was the Hutchins' rig, but the Negro cowboy was driving the wagon.

"Where's . . . ?" That's when I spotted the canvas tarp in the back seat.

"Caleb, run up to the house and fetch Frank," Rex told me.

I didn't have to, because the barking dogs had alerted the captain, and he was making a beeline toward us as Old George stopped the team.

Now a Michigan surrey isn't a good wagon for transporting two bodies. Plus detectives, trackers and lawyers would have complained that Old George should have left the dead men where he had found them, but Old George didn't think that Christian, didn't want wolves and ravens to get at Judge and Fred Hutchins, so he had dragged them into the buggy and covered them with the tarp. When he pulled back the canvas to show the captain, I saw Fred Hutchins's face. He had always been so ruddy, so wind-burned, but in death looked so pale, and the bloody hole in his forehead sickened me. I didn't see Judge's body, having turned around to grip the fence rail for support.

"How did it happen?" the captain asked.

"I don't know, sir," Old George replied. "I saw the vultures. Thought it might have been where a wolf got a calf or somethin'. Near Walnut Draw I guess they surprised rustlers. Least, some cattle had been held there, and they was all gone when I rode up."

"And?"

"Well, best I can tell, sir, Mister Fred and Judge, they must have seen smoke from a fire, maybe heard the beef a-bawlin', 'cause they left this buggy about a quarter mile down the trail. Judge, I think he took a rifle, tried to sneak around the camp, flank them boys, I guess. They put up a fight. Judge, he caught two bullets in his back. Mister Fred, he got belly-shot. From the blood, I think he was a-tryin' to crawl back to the wagon, but they run him down. Then they up and shot Mister Fred in the head. I'm . . . I'm right sorry, Capt'n."

The captain didn't reply.

Chapter Seventeen

The undertaker in Roswell took care of the bodies of Fred and Judge Hutchins as best he could, laying them out in the finest coffins available, and loading them into the back of a buckboard for transport to Puerto de Luna. Gray clouds threatened rain every day we rode north on that desolate stretch of wagon road, which paralleled the west bank of the Pecos River, but the storm never unleashed its fury, just darkened and chilled our moods with gloom.

I had assumed the brothers would be buried somewhere on their ranch, or maybe in the Masonic Cemetery in Las Cruces, but Judge Hutchins's wife—Fred had never married—had been buried fifteen years earlier in Puerto de Luna, so our somber escorts hauled the coffins there.

At least I'd get to see Grandma Anna once more.

Rex Steele drove the buckboard, and I rode with him. Flanking us on horseback were Jesús Salazar and Jim Park, foreman of the H-Bar, with Old George and H-Bar hand Nels Iverson, riding drag. The captain, of course, pointed our way, and another rider kept shadowing us, sometimes riding ahead, sometimes talking to the captain, often dropping well behind us, and every once in a while pulling up alongside the wagon to, I guess, vex me. He never spent much time with us, though, even when we made camp, which suited me just fine.

Besides, Slim Reed had never been a friend to Judge or Mr. Fred. Only reason he accompanied us was because the association had called a major meeting in Puerto de Luna the afternoon of the funeral Mass.

Another meeting! The thought must have disgusted the captain, and I remembered Fred Hutchins complaining: *You can bullyrag these vermin only so many times, and if the threats don't take, it's time for action.* My uncle, I could feel, must have thought the same thing, especially now. Once he had voiced a similar complaint to Albert Fountain. Now Fountain and little Henry were dead, and so were Judge and Fred Hutchins. Not to mention the men Slim Reed had gunned down.

If you could have seen the faces of the riders on that trip, you might have thought we were riding to the gallows, our own gallows, and that's pretty much how we felt, but my spirits were soon lifted after we forded the Pecos at a bend in the river near Fort Sumner.

Rex pointed out the walled cemetery, said that's where Billy the Kid was buried, but we didn't stop. Wasn't much of a cemetery, not by St. Louis standards, but Fort Sumner wasn't much of a fort. Fact is, it wasn't a fort, not any more, hadn't been for years, although the buildings still stood, barracks turned into hotels, homes, saloons, and barns. Really the town wasn't much more than what Rex Steele or Dickie Fergusson would call a wide spot in a small road.

What took my mind off the deaths, and Slim Reed, was when Rex told me that Juan Patrón, an old friend of the Kid, was buried underneath the floor of the Puerto de Luna church. You know how Rex was. When I hadn't shown much interest in Billy the Kid's grave, he had to think of something else to say, so he brought up Juan Patrón. And you know what? I found that much more interesting that the final resting place of Billy the Kid. Buried inside a church? That fascinated a fourteen-year-old Methodist.

North of Fort Sumner, the country changed from the endless expanse of the Llano Escatado ruled by the harsh wind, sand, and biting insects. That lifted my spirits, too, and the skies eventually lightened.

We wound down into a red-rocked valley, lush and verdant, perhaps the most beautiful part of the territory I'd seen since Glorieta. Pretty it was, Puerto de Luna, but back then they used to say that anything went in this town. Comancheros used to ply their trade, but things had turned quieter by 1896, though I had heard the H-Bar hands whispering that the town butcher and a few other unsavory characters in town weren't too particular from whom they bought their cattle.

Me? I hadn't seen any signs of rustlers. Mostly what I saw had been the sheepherder camps dotting the countryside, and about all I could hear were ewes and lambs crying. The town itself looked small, quaint. It had become seat of the new Guadalupe County five years earlier, and was dominated by a two-story courthouse made of hand-hewn rock that sat on one side of the Las Vegas Road, and the Nuestra Señora de Refugio

Catholic Church on the other. We turned left toward the church, but, trailing Captain Hart, made another left turn away from the pretty red-stone church and followed a narrow, muddy street to a long adobe building surrounded by shade trees, decrepit fence, goats and chickens.

"What's this?" I asked Rex.

"Grzelachowski's store," he answered, and my spirits became their brightest when Grandma Anna stepped out to greet us, smiling the way only a grandmother can while shouting at the chickens to stop their squawking. Naturally the chickens didn't obey her commands.

A lanky man, better than six-foot-six in his stovepipe boots, stepped out beside her. He sported a waxed mustache and a weary face while nervously fingering the curled brim of his derby before settling the hat over his graying hair.

"You'll stay here with your grandma," the captain told me. "Till the funeral."

Still staring at the stranger, I hopped off the wagon, and just stood there like an oaf, not knowing what to do.

"Is Harrigan here?" the captain addressed the tall man.

"Well, I ain't seen him," the man answered in a thick Southern drawl.

"You figure to find a murderer at a funeral, Garrett?" Slim Reed's icy voice unnerved me, reminding me of his presence and spoiling my good mood. It didn't seem to help the tall man's disposition, either.

The tall man pulled back his broadcloth coat, at first I thought to reveal the dull star pinned to the lapel of his matching vest, but then I spotted the long-barreled Colt holstered high on his right hip. "Well, I see one already," Pat Garrett answered with a voice equally cold, staring directly at Slim Reed.

Reed grinned. "Likewise. 'Course, Slim Reed never killed no pal."

"You never had one."

The next words were the sternest, and they came from neither Slim Reed nor Pat Garrett. For that matter, even Captain Hart remained silent.

"You two scalawags watch your tongues," Grandma Anna said. "Two brave men lie in the back of that wagon, this is a funeral, and I won't stand for no disrespect. Not in my front yard, no, sir."

A nod from the captain sent Rex backing up the team and turning around the buckboard, then heading toward the church. The men, including Pat Garrett and Slim Reed, followed, leaving me standing among chickens and a calico cat, which had suddenly appeared, purring gently and almost tripping me. I tried to look properly somber in front of my grandmother. Somewhere inside the store, a clock chimed, and Grandma Anna announced: "Funeral will start in an hour. That'll give you plenty of time to tell me what in blazes happened to your arm, you po' child. Come on inside, Caleb. I made something cool to drink."

No need to tell you-all about the funeral or the burial service in the nearby cemetery. It was the first Catholic ceremony I ever attended, and I have to say it pretty much frightened me. I just sat rigid, sweating and itching but daring not to move, even though I really wanted to see that grave of Juan Patrón but couldn't see much over the black-veiled hats of the ladies and bowed heads of the men. Afterward, the men folk filed off across the road toward the courthouse for the big association meeting, Grandma Anna walked with some ladies to another adobe building, and I wandered off to the corral and livery, exploring Puerto de Luna.

But only briefly.

When I saw the priest talking to a gray-haired Mexican woman outside a café, I figured the Nuestra Señora de Refugio church had to be empty, I wandered back toward the church, across the plaza, and, making sure nobody saw me, through the front doors, determined to find that grave.

Now, I can't tell you what I expected to find. Tombstone in the middle of one of the floor tiles? Maybe a crypt? Who knows? I sure didn't expect to see Mary Magdalene Holliday standing near the fountain of Holy Water.

"What are you doing here?"

She whirled, started to bring up the Winchester—which I hadn't noticed until then—but stopped.

The sight of a weapon in a house of worship shocked and offended my religious upbringing, and I shouted: "You don't bring a rifle into a church!"

"I ain't exactly a practicing Catholic." Slowly a smile appeared, but she walked past me to the heavy doors, looking left and right, before stepping back and pulling the doors shut. The church darkened except for the fading light creeping through tall, stained-glass windows.

"How's your arm?" she asked, and I forgot all about the Winchester, even forgot about Juan Patrón.

"It's better."

"That sorrel widow-maker bucked you off again?"

My head dropped, and oddly enough I felt tears welling as I thought about Chuck. "Uh . . . the captain . . . he killed him."

Mary snorted. "That figures."

"Well . . . why are you here?"

"Ain't you the nosy one. Had business in town. Figured I'd pay some respects. . . ." Now it was Mary who struggled for words. She shifted the rifle in her hands, looked at her muddy boots, and finally explained: "Judge was my godfather . . . or was supposed to be . . . long time ago."

When I offered my condolences, she grunted again. "I shouldn't have come," she said.

I wanted to tell her that I was right pleased she had, but instead, just to say something, anything to stop Mary from retreating and disappearing, I offered: "Times are bad."

"Ain't nothing different." When her eyes fell on the Holy Water, she let out a laugh and shook her head. "Old habits," she said without mirth, dipping her fingers and crossing herself.

Suddenly the front door swung open, the Winchester barrel swung up, and Mary Holliday pushed me aside, pushed me to the floor, her strength, her quickness surprising me.

"Child," Grandma Anna barked as she stepped into the church, "you put that rifle down. I ought to tan your hide for such sacrilege."

Mary started to talk back, but I guess she thought better of it, because she started to lower the rifle, only then her eyes widened as Rex Steele stepped up behind my grandmother. The loud metallic noise of the lever mechanism propelled me into action, and, still on my knees, I launched myself into a dive for the rifle with a scream—"NO!"—fearing Mary would kill Grandma Anna by mistake. All I did was skin my good elbow crashing against the tile, missing Mary and her Winchester completely, but at least breaking my fall and not crushing my broken arm.

As I skidded across the rough tile, I heard Rex's voice: "Don't be a fool, Mary!"

Silence. I knew Mary hadn't pulled the trigger. Face flushing, I sat up, catching my breath while repositioning my cast in my sling made from Mary's bandanna. Mary still gripped the rifle, but held it across her waist, the barrel pointed toward the stained-glass window. She and Rex glared at each other while Grandma Anna, who looked suddenly pale, helped me to my feet, and she asked about my arm.

Before I could answer that I was fine, Rex began challenging Mary. "Ten head of cattle are in that corral, Mary," Rex told her. "And an almighty poor job of altering Hart brands."

I had seen those cattle, but hadn't paid much attention to the brands. Suddenly it became clear to me that Rex and Mary knew each other, fairly well, I could guess, and Grandma Anna knew her, too, for, upon hearing Rex's charges, she began to scold Mary.

"Oh, shut up," Mary snapped. "The both of you." She looked at me, too, without any love in her eyes, and I noticed her trembling. "I'll be taking my leave."

"You'd best," Rex said. "Slim Reed's here. Harrigan, too, and Salazar saw those cattle you stole. He's probably telling Frank right now." He shook his head in disgust. "Stealing from Frank's one thing, but I thought you'd have a little more character than to bring them here, when they're burying Fred and Judge, knowing Frank and every other rancher would be here. I. . . ."

"Reckon you mistook your man." Mary was clenching the rifle so tightly her knuckles had turned white.

Rex appeared just as angry. He pushed his hat back, those friendly eyes flaming with rage, and I realized he stood shaking, too, but when he tried to resume his tirade, Mary silenced him.

"I don't need you preaching to me," she snapped, and, as a warning to Grandma Anna, added: "You, neither."

"Just get on your horse and light a shuck," Rex said. "And don't expect me to protect you no more."

"Like you ever. . . ."

"Enough!" Grandma Anna thundered in a voice you wouldn't expect from a woman of her age. "Not in a house of the Lord." I worried that the priest or an altar boy would hear the arguing, come rushing back into the church, or worse yet, since nobody had bothered to close the doors after Grandma Anna and Rex appeared, that Slim Reed, Pat Garrett, or Captain Hart would come investigate. Grandma Anna must have had similar fears because she stepped aside, looked over her shoulder and outside.

I heard horses, muffled voices of men, but nothing that alarmed me. Grandma Anna let out a sigh, and, reaching out, she grabbed the iron pull on the heavy door. It closed again, but not all the way, for the wind moaned ominously through a crack. "Go out the back door, dear," she told Mary, her voice full of urgency but not panic. "Be careful, and stay clear of Chavez's corral."

With an oath, Mary whirled, but she did look at me. "You all right?" she asked.

"Yeah."

"You children," Grandma Anna said, her eyes tearing as she looked at Mary and me. "You ever get into trouble, bad trouble, I want you to know that I'm always here for you . . . the both of you . . . especially. You remember that. Both of you. Any time. Any. . . ." Something caught in her throat, and she turned away, heading outside but talking over her shoulder. "Rex, we'd best leave now."

Light spilled through the open doorway, and I could see several men on the streets, and many, many more out by the courthouse. No one paid much attention to my grandmother as she walked across the plaza, and the men at the courthouse were too far away, too preoccupied in their conversations, to notice anything out of the ordinary at the church.

"Come on, Caleb," Rex said. Neither his tone nor his stance had softened any. He glared at Mary. "And you . . . we're done, gal."

"We've been done, Steele," Mary shot out. "You think I've forgotten you was there with that high-and-mighty Frank Hart when y'all hanged my husband?"

"He wasn't no husband," Rex said. "You didn't marry him for love, but spite." She was walking away, heading down the center aisle, toward the back door behind the pulpit, but Rex kept talking, though he never raised his voice.

"How many times did that sorry cuss put you in the El Paso hospital? How many times did he beat you? He would have killed you, gal, just like he killed Colby King." She had reached the door. "Frank done you a favor."

Mary spun around. "I never asked for no favors . . . especially from him." She spit on the floor before darting outside.

Chapter Eighteen

Captain Hart's Vengeance Raid.

That's what the Santa Fé *New Mexican*, the Río Grande *Republican*, and the El Paso *Daily Herald* would all eventually come to call it, although I'm not certain as to which newspaper thought up the title first, but it stuck around for a few years until, like the captain himself, it slowly faded from people's consciousness.

I never really thought of it as a raid. I mean raids were events like Quantrill's sacking Lawrence, Kansas, or Apache uprisings, things like that, and, although outraged at the deaths of the Hutchins brothers, I'm not sure vengeance had that much to do with the decision of the Southeastern New Mexico Stock Growers' Association. Tired of losing livestock, the ranchers just felt frustrated. Besides, from the newspaper stories I read around that time, the captain didn't say a word during the association meeting after the double funeral in Puerto de Luna, but Franklin J. Hart would get the credit, and the blame, for that raid when association members decided to take matters into their own hands.

Some say they had Pat Garrett's blessing, but I don't know that for a fact. Garrett had been at the funeral, and maybe at the meeting—never could figure that out for myself—but he kept his focus on building a case against the men who had murdered the Fountains, and many folks in the territory complained that he took too much time doing that. Some even suggested he was scared. Well, people talk. Personally I think Garrett just let the cattlemen mete out their brand of justice as long as it got the support of Republican newspapers and lawmakers in Santa Fé. Maybe he hoped these "raiders" would flush out the killers of Colonel Fountain and Henry. ¿Quién sabe?

Still, I've often thought that there wouldn't have been a Vengeance Raid—I'll bow to the old newspapers for lack of a better phrase—if it hadn't been for the deaths of the Fountains. Back at the bunkhouse after the funeral, I overheard a conversation between Hobbs Wallace and Rex Steele. The death of Colonel Fountain and little Henry had been the primer, Hobbs had said, the other incidents just added to the cauldron, and the killings of the Hutchins brothers boiled the pot over. It made sense to me back then, and it still does. Of course, things might have boiled over anyway.

Mary Holliday sure didn't help matters.

Jesús Salazar had informed the captain of the stolen livestock in Chavez's corral, but Mary had sneaked out of town, and so had Ramón Chavez, for that matter. Word soon spread that once Chavez, a butcher known for doing business with rustlers, heard what had come out of the association meeting, he pulled up stakes and lit out for Trinidad, Colorado. Anyway, some Double Diamond boys, in town for the association meeting, agreed to drive the stolen livestock back to Hart range while the rest of us rode for home, covering the distance in half the time it took us to ride up to Puerto de Luna.

No one talked much on the journey south, but I guess all of us knew what had been decided at the meeting even before the captain confirmed the rumors at the bunkhouse the night we reached headquarters. Word had spread to every Hart line shack and branding outfit, because I had never seen so many Hart riders at one place. Men I hadn't seen since first arriving in the territory, and even more that I'd never seen.

Hobbs Wallace grumbled about having to cook for so many men on such short notice, but I think he liked the chore, liked the chance to please so many cowboys. I even saw him smiling once before Captain Hart started his speech.

"It's war," the captain announced. "We're done mollycoddling these vermin. Anybody who ain't up to making a stand, ain't ready to be shot at or to shoot at someone, you can draw your time. I won't begrudge none of you."

Kim Harrigan had come home with us, and, squatting in the middle of the bunkhouse floor, surrounded by Hart riders, I sought him out, waiting for him to step forward, but he just sat in a chair near the stove, cleaning his fingernails with a knife blade. A couple of hands, young men scarcely older than me, did quit, and, true to his word, Captain Hart paid them in full, even shook their hands. He said he'd put in a word for them if they wanted a job at one of the other outfits recognized by the association, but both boys shook their heads. One said he would try Arizona, and the other said his cousin in Del Río had promised him a job. Sitting on his bunk, Manuel hesitated, once started to stand, but sank back onto the cot. I felt eyes from all directions burning through my soul, although Captain Hart never glanced in my direction, but I kept my crossed legs locked, boots planted to the floor, and tried to look strong and determined.

"Anybody else?" the captain asked, but an uneasy silence filled the bunkhouse after the two men had left.

"All right," my uncle eventually said. "Here's the way it'll work. And what I say tonight stays in this bunkhouse. It ain't to be discussed over cards in some dram shop."

The association had formed a militia, electing Captain Hart "colonel" based on his experience riding with the Mesilla Scouts back in the 1880s. Four armed "regiments" would ride across the Tularosa Basin, one led by Captain Hart, another with a rancher near Piños Wells named Rosecrans in charge, a third led by H-Bar foreman, Jim Park, and the fourth commanded by a Tularosa rancher named Gabaldón. These regiments could divide up as necessary, keeping a minimum of fifteen riders in each raiding party. That way, they'd be sure to overwhelm most thieves they came across. Rustlers, or suspected rustlers, were to be driven out of the territory and "encouraged" to stay out, turned in to local law enforcement, or, if deemed prudent, executed.

None of that was ever put down in writing.

"Any questions?" the captain asked after spilling out the plan.

"What about Oliver Lee?" Old George asked. "We going after him?"

"That's up to José Gabaldón," the captain answered, "if Lee's caught rustling, or if any of his riders are caught. Don't fret over Lee, or Gilliland. They ain't our responsibility. Lee's in Gabaldón's territory, and José's a good man. We'll be responsible for our range from White Oaks to the Texas border, and as far south as H-Bar range. Anything else?"

Dickie Fergusson shuffled his feet, started to ask something, stopped, then finally got up his nerve. "Say we catch some rustlers. Who decides if we . . . well, who hands out the death sentence?"

"I do." That came as no surprise. "The association decided the leaders of each vigilance committee would be judge, jury, and, if needed, hangman. If you sign on, you agree to this. Anyone who can't stomach that . . . well, that's why I'm giving you a choice. Quit now, because, once we ride, there ain't no quitting."

Outside a coyote began yipping, answered by dozens of other coyotes. It sounded like they were all laughing at us, and that really pricked my nerves. Part of me wanted to bolt out of the bunkhouse door, to run back to St. Louis, but I made myself stay. I had to.

"It ain't no church social." Captain Hart sounded as though he was talking directly to me, but I just stared at the bunkhouse floor. "Some of you rode with me when we caught up with Colby King's killer. Some of you might remember Ab Northrup, and I ain't ashamed of what happened. This here deal might come to nothing. Rustlers might run out, and those we catch should have better sense than to put up a fight. Only you can't count on that. We might find some men that need killing, because I ain't one to leave the killers of Judge and Fred Hutchins to the law of this territory. We've seen too many of those scoundrels set free. But it ain't an easy thing . . . killing . . . it eats at one's innards like bad whiskey. So if you can't stomach killing, the door's still open."

No one spoke for the longest time, and, to my surprise, no one left. "All right," the captain said, standing and patting his pockets in search of his pipe and tobacco. "We ride at first light."

Voices erupted, and cowboys began talking amongst themselves while Hobbs Wallace announced that supper would be served in five minutes. I pushed my way toward the door, snaking between bodies, smelling smoke, sweat, and leather, feeling one old-timer slap my back as he told me that I had plenty of grit, that he was right proud of me. I moved through the ocean of men, trying to find Kim Harrigan, but he had stepped into the darkness, and I followed him outside. Maybe he's leaving, I thought, only didn't want to walk out in front of the boys, quitting like that. I stared into the shadows of the barn and corral. No, Kim wouldn't do that. Sneaking out, that's not his style. Most likely, he was just answering nature's call.

Stumbling around, I decided to stay outside for fresh air, but when I smelled pipe smoke, my head shot up. Captain Hart stood leaning against the bunkhouse wall, standing next to Rex Steele, busy rolling a cigarette.

When my uncle called out my name, my stomach began dancing again.

My voice cracked when I answered: "Sir?"

"You'll stay here with Hobbs. We'll have crews coming in and out, and he'll need the help."

Well, the relief I felt didn't last long, for something told me that staying put was wrong. I thought my nerves would fail me, that I would simply nod and say "Yes, sir." The voice that answered Captain Hart didn't sound like mine at all.

"Reckon I'll be riding with you."

It was only when the captain lowered his pipe, his wolf eyes blazing, that I really understood that, indeed, I had spoken those words of defiance.

"No, you ain't," he snapped back.

"I am," I said, quickly adding: "sir."

Now, I don't know why I said that. I had come West seeking adventure, or so I had dreamed back in Missouri, and riding on a vengeance raid, chasing rustlers, well, that sure had the elements a kid could find in any yellow-back novel, but I didn't think that's why I was making my stand.

"I wouldn't be so jo-fired about taking part in this deal," Captain Hart said. "I sure ain't." He cursed, tapping his pipe against the adobe until the embers glowed again. "Them boys that rode out, you ask me, they showed good sense."

"I'm riding with you." I made myself look in his eyes, and refused to turn away when those yellow-gray eyes blazed. "I'm a Hart," I said.

Maybe it had to do with blood, maybe not. I don't think I was bragging, trying to prove myself, but something kept telling me that I had to ride with the captain. For my sake. For Mary Magdalene Holliday's sake. Criminy, for Captain Hart's sake.

He smoked his pipe, staring at me, and at last nodded. "Suit yourself," he said, but his eyes seemed to lose their harshness, and, before he stepped off the porch and walked through the darkness toward his house, he put his right hand on my good shoulder. The squeeze was only slight, as was his nod of support.

You'd think I would have been staggered with pride, like I had taken my first step toward manhood, but I didn't feel very proud, and I sure didn't feel like a man. What I guess I felt was, well, numb. I stood there next to Rex Steele, wondering what I was getting myself into, wondering why I had demanded to ride with these men.

Rex lit his cigarette and grinned at me. Although I had scores of questions for him, we hadn't spoken since that evening in the Nuestra Señora de Refugio Catholic Church. I hadn't had the opportunity, or heart, or courage to talk, for as soon as we had left the church, Nels Iverson of the H-Bar had run up to us, peppering Rex with questions and rumors about everything going on at the association meeting and Jesús Salazar's discovery of stolen cattle at the butcher's corral, while Grandma Anna called me away to escort her back to her home. For that matter, Grandma Anna and I hadn't talked things over, either. Saying she felt dead on her feet, she went to lie down in bed, and, a few minutes later, Captain Hart and the boys rode up and announced we were going home.

Now Rex took a long drag on the cigarette. He also reached out to grip my shoulder and give me that fatherly nod.

"You're becoming a son to him," he said fondly before looking toward the hilltop where that mysterious grave stood somewhere in the darkness.

"Can't tell you how that gladdens my heart because . . . well. . . ." Another drag on the smoke. Then, from inside the bunkhouse, Hobbs Wallace bellowed out that supper was ready.

Neither of us moved toward the door. Rex blew out a stream of smoke and spoke softly. "But you shouldn't ride with us tomorrow."

"I have to go."

His head bobbed again, and I realized I wasn't looking at the typical big, wide Rex Steele grin underneath that pulled-low hat. This smile held sadness, not humor. I think Rex knew why I had decided to ride with the captain even before I did.

"I'd stay clear of her, Caleb." He flicked his cigarette into the night. "She's . . . well . . . don't come between her and Frank."

That was it. That was my reason, my determination. I had to protect Mary Holliday. That's exactly what I had to do, why I had to become one of Captain Hart's raiders.

I recalled Mary, Rex, and their bitter exchange back inside the Puerto de Luna church, and I needed an answer to this notion that had come upon me.

"Is she . . . is Mary your daughter?" I asked.

"She's Frank's daughter, Caleb," he answered quickly, as if he had anticipated the question. "I figured you knew that already. She didn't tell you?"

"Well . . ."—my head shook—"not in so many words." Looking back on it, I thought maybe she had told me, but I hadn't listened. We both started to speak at the same time, instantly stopping when Old George and another Negro cowhand walked outside, chewing on biscuits as they made their way toward the privy, talking about horses. They only gave us casual nods before the blackness swallowed them. I found myself looking in the direction of that hilltop grave.

"You ought to stay put," Rex said again. "Chances are she pulled out of the territory after Puerto de Luna. Chances are she ran off to Tascosa. She would . . . if she's smart."

I wondered how much he knew about Mary and me—not that there was much to tell—wondered if Kim Harrigan had told Rex anything. Probably not, but Kim had told the captain about running into Mary that time in the Capitans, which seemed years ago, and Rex Steele had the captain's ear, folks said. After all, he was the Hart foreman.

Spurs sang out a tune, and we turned toward the footfalls as Kim Harrigan stepped onto the porch. Harrigan spit tobacco juice into a crack and shot us a curious look.

"Caleb will be riding with us," Rex announced, his words lacking emotion.

"Suit yourself," Harrigan told me, in no mood for conversation, and walked inside the noisy bunkhouse. Rex followed him, not looking back at me as he said: "Remember what I said, Caleb. Mary's no good, and I've known her longer than you. She's bent on bringing herself down to see Satan himself. Don't let her bring you down with her."

I just stood there, leaning against the wall for support, trying to sort out all I had just learned. Mary was Frank Hart's daughter, and Frank Hart had hanged her husband. Why? I knew most of the facts, but I just couldn't see how anything like that could ever happen. I wondered what Grandma Anna thought about this horrible family tragedy, recalling the way she had looked at Mary back inside the church, the sadness, the longing deep in her old, weary eyes.

Hobbs Wallace stuck his head out the doorway, looked to and fro, found me, and said with a snarl: "Best come inside and eat, boy, before I throw all this slop out to the dogs!"

Well, I didn't feel hungry, don't think I ate a bite, and I sure didn't sleep well that night.

Chapter Nineteen

Thunder rumbled in the distance that morning as we divided into groups before leaving Hart headquarters. We didn't even have to wait on Dickie Fergusson. Fact is, he had left the bunkhouse before Hobbs Wallace had the coffee boiling, and I found him brushing horses when the rest of us left for the barn and corral. He even helped bridle and saddle my mare, and spoke scarcely a word as he went about his chores.

Nervous, he was trying to keep busy, and he wasn't alone. I doubt if I heard more than a dozen words over breakfast, and even less in the corral, especially once Captain Hart came down from his house, carrying a shotgun and box of shells.

"You clean your revolver?" the captain asked me.

"No, sir," I stammered. "I mean . . . not lately."

I still had the Harrington & Richardson .32 holstered in my gun belt. It had taken a pounding when Chuck had thrown me while chasing Tim Sutton, clogging the barrel and caking the cylinder with dirt, and Kim Harrigan had cleaned and oiled it for me at the bunkhouse. I hadn't fired it, though, really hadn't thought much about it.

The captain grunted. "Is it loaded?"

"Yes, sir."

"Good, unbuckle your belt and give it to Old

George yonder. He don't have no six-shooter, and I'd feel better with him holding it than you, in case we do run into any trouble."

Well, that eased the tension some, caused a handful of the boys to chuckle, and Rex slapped the brim of my hat good-naturedly as, red-faced, I removed my weapon, sliding my left arm out of the bandanna sling and using my fingers to help unfasten the buckle and wrap the belt around the holster before passing my rig to the one-eyed Negro cowhand, who took it without comment and buckled it around his slim waist.

"Hart riders don't pout," the captain barked, which sparked even more nervous laughter. Suddenly he shoved the double-barrel shotgun he held into my good hand. "Here," he said. "Slide that into your scabbard, and watch it, it's loaded with buckshot."

The shotgun was a twelve-gauge U.S. Arms model with long barrels of Damascus steel, much heavier than I had expected. It took all my effort to shove it in the scabbard, being one-handed and all.

"That's a lot of weapon for a kid with a broken arm," said Hobbs Wallace, who had come out from the bunkhouse to pass us all sacks of food, beef jerky, and corn dodgers. I put my sack, along with a box of shells my uncle gave me, in the saddlebags. Rex and some of the other hands just smiled at the cook's observation, but I knew that's why the captain had given me the twelve-gauge. It was too much weapon for me.

With my left forearm still in a hard, dirty cast, I could never bring that shotgun to my shoulder and fire, not accurately. The kick from the buckshot would knock me on my backside, and, providing I didn't accidentally shoot one of my friends, the Hart riders would be howling with laughter at me—if it ever came to a shooting, that is.

Which, as the days wore on, became less and less likely.

Oh, we covered some territory. Wore out some horses. Threw some shoes. Yet we didn't come across any rustlers or suspected rustlers, at least, not at first.

In my place, Manuel had been left behind to help Hobbs Wallace with the cooking, and I remember him crossing himself when we rode back to headquarters after a fruitless first day on the trail. Relief splashed across his face when Jesús Salazar told him we had seen no one. We were the second group to arrive back at the ranch; the first one had been as luckless as we had been. Or maybe I should say as lucky as we had been. The other two groups rode up later in the evening with similar results.

The next night, we camped on the trail after finding only Hart cattle, although we did cut some sign, which may or may not have been rustlers. In any event, Kim Harrigan lost the trail at a muddy creek. We ran a cold camp that night and, the next morning, cut a wide loop southeast, trying to find the trail, but managed to scare up only some antelope and jack rabbits. On the third day, we met a Double Diamond rider who had been sent out by Jim Park as a messenger.

Park's H-Bar riders had captured one stranger, but couldn't convince themselves that he was a rustler, though he did arouse their suspicions. So they bruised him a little, threatened to hang him anyway, then put him in his saddle, slapped the rump of his gelding, and fired a few shots over his head to persuade him to find a more inviting place to hang his hat. Rosecrans had burned down a couple of shacks where they found running irons and the remnants of a butchered Rocking R hide that rustlers had tried to burn. No one had heard from José Gabaldón.

"But the way I got things figgered," the H-Bar rider told Captain Hart, "if that ol' Mex had come across anyone or pulled a trigger, we'd have heard somethin'. Anyway, Jim Park sent me out to find out what you've seen or done."

"Nothing," the captain said, more grunt than word.

"How 'bout any of your other outfits?"

The captain's head shook slightly, and he kicked his feet out of both stirrups to stretch his legs while gripping the saddle horn. "Cut a trail a while back, but lost it." He shook his head and swore. "For all I know, it was my own men." He spit out tobacco juice. "I sent some boys over to Los Portales, told them to check those caves where the Kid used to hide out," Captain Hart continued. "I'm going to take this crew back to the ranch, get us some fresh mounts, maybe ride over to the Texas border myself."

The rider nodded. "How 'bout Slim Reed? You heard from him?"

Reed, the way I understood things, had been given plenty of rein during the Vengeance Raid, told to cover whatever ground he wanted as a scout and hunter, and, if he came across a rustler camp or trail, he could find the nearest raiding party. I figured he got sent out alone because nobody wanted him with them. Well, that's what I wanted to believe.

"Nothing," the captain answered.

"All right," the H-Bar man said. "I'll tell Jimmy what you tol' me, an' we'll send word if we find anybody or hear more news. Good huntin'!"

"Yeah," the captain said wearily as the H-Bar rider kicked his mount into a trot and rode away.

The way things turned out, the captain's men did find some rustlers around Los Portales, spilling the first blood of Captain Hart's Vengeance Raid. One Hart rider got his little finger shot off, and one rustler was killed. Another rustler was wounded in the thigh—a doctor wound up sawing off his leg— and the other two rustlers surrendered after being promised they wouldn't be hanged. Hart riders are men of their word, and the rustlers were turned over to the law in Puerto de Luna.

That bit of news we wouldn't learn until later. Shortly after the H-Bar cowhand left, we turned back for the Hart Ranch, and I was mighty glad. I had exchanged Penny for a buckskin, not knowing the gelding had a pounding gate, so I was happy to see Penny in the corral when we rode up in the late afternoon in a drizzling rain. When we rode out again, I'd be riding Penny. I was even happier to see Rex Steele's favorite horse grazing nearby, for that meant Rex and his party had ridden back, too, so I'd have him and Dickie Fergusson to talk to in the bunkhouse that night.

My spirits dimmed when a man stepped out of the barn. At first I thought it was Manuel, until I saw the big cigar and dirty denim clothes.

"Was hoping you'd show up shortly," Slim

Reed addressed my uncle. He flicked ash from the cigar and smiled. "Slim Reed found us some game."

Naturally I wasn't privy to the rest of the conversation between Reed, the captain, and Rex Steele. We rubbed down our horses, then grained and watered them before drifting up to the bunkhouse for hot coffee and to get out of our wet duds. No doubt, we all looked forward to sleeping under a roof, but that wouldn't happen. Thirty minutes later, the captain walked in, announcing: "Finish your coffee. We're lighting a shuck."

That was one miserable ride as the rain never stopped. Never turned loose, just kept drizzling as we rode toward Lincoln. We made camp on the Río Bonito well before dawn, another cold camp, and split up into two parties around daybreak. Rex Steele took Reed with his group, and they headed down the Bonito toward the camp Reed said he had found. The captain would lead our men southeast, a flanking maneuver, they called it.

Well, it didn't quite work out that way. Long around noon, we heard muffled gunshots, and the captain swore. Rex and Reed had moved in too soon, we thought, so we spurred our horses and galloped over juniper-dotted hills. By the time we got there, though, the fight was over, and two men lay dead, rivulets of blood flowing into puddles of water.

First thing I saw, though, wasn't the gut-shot bodies of two Mexicans. No, it was Mary Holliday's big dun horse. A couple of seconds later, my eyes found Mary, about the time Slim Reed cuffed her to the ground.

"Reed!" the captain roared, and the gunman whirled, his right hand racing for his revolver.

"Lay a hand on her again. . . ." The captain didn't finish, didn't need to, because Reed moved his hand away from his gun. Rex Steele helped Mary to her feet, but she pulled away from him and dabbed her busted lip, eyes full of fear and hatred.

"We come up on 'em," Reed said. "Looked like they was about to light out, so I figured it best to stop them. Give 'em a chance, but that greaser, yonder, pulled his pistol."

Dickie Fergusson's head bowed, his words barely audible. "That ain't exactly how it happened."

A cruel grin stretched across Reed's bronzed face. "Well, it's how Slim Reed saw things, bucko."

"Any cattle?" Captain Hart asked. "Hides?

"Not that I've seen, Frank," Rex answered, "but running irons. And. . . ." He gave Mary a sad look and shook his head. "Well, you know her."

I've often wondered how Mary felt all that time, staring up at better than thirty Hart riders and a killer like Slim Reed, facing her father for the first time in I don't know how long, and all this after seeing two companions shot down before her eyes. Later, I'd learn that Slim Reed had done all the shooting, and Dickie said he might have shot Mary, too, had Rex Steele not slammed his galloping horse into Reed's bay gelding. The two Mexicans I had never seen until that day, but I don't reckon I'll ever forget their faces, frozen in death. Boys they were, somewhere in age between me and Mary Holliday, dark eyes staring without seeing, mouths locked in the screams during their death throes. Wish I could forget them, but I can't, although I'm glad I had no hand in their deaths. Mary had been reaching for her Winchester, planning on dying game with her two friends, but Old George had thrown a loop over her shoulders and pulled tight. Not knowing then that she was a woman, Old George said he thought about using my .32, but trusted his lariat more than my little revolver. I'm glad of that, although Mary wasn't about to quit. She freed herself before the old cowhand could wrap a dally around his horn, her speed surprising the raiders, and was crawling for the rifle when Jesús Salazar stepped on it and leveled his rusty old Navy at her head, muttering a prayer for her to stop.

She had, but only with great reluctance.

'Course, I don't think that should surprise any of you-all, I mean, about finding Mary Holliday in that nest of thieves. Doubt I would be telling this story if we hadn't met up like that. All during those days since Puerto de Luna, I felt it would come to this. Knew it more than felt it. That's why I had insisted on riding with the captain, and I'm glad I was with Captain Hart on that day and not riding from Los Portales to Puerto de Luna with one dead rustler and three prisoners.

What I didn't expect was the watch. I had slowly dismounted, ground-reined Penny, and found myself walking to help Mary, although I didn't know exactly what I could do. I was probably just a few feet from Reed and Mary when the captain spoke again.

"Rex," he said, refusing to look at his daughter, "we'll bury them two boys. You and Reed take . . .

her . . . take her to Lincoln, hand her over to Justice Sanchez."

"Lincoln!" Reed said with a sneer. "The Lincoln jail can't hold a cripple."

"You've earned your bonus, Reed," Captain Hart said icily.

"That ain't enough for the likes of her, woman or not. Because old Slim Reed, me, took this off that *puta!*"

Captain Hart's wolf eyes went mad, and, when he swung down from his horse, I think he planned on tearing Slim Reed apart. Rex Steele must have read the same intention, because he was moving quickly, racing to stop someone, the captain or Reed, from getting killed. The captain stopped, though, when he saw the watch hanging from the chain in Reed's outstretched left hand.

Yeah, as close as I stood to Slim Reed, I remembered that watch. The fourteen-karat gold case glinted as it spun on the heavy chain, catching the few rays of light that shot through the purple and gray clouds. A seventeen-jewel Waltham Vanguard, with a bridled horse's head engraved on the case, tall spruce trees, and a fence in the background, several floral designs underneath. I had lost count of the times I had seen Judge Hutchins taking that watch from his vest pocket, absentmindedly winding it while talking about some important matters.

My stomach turned over, and my knees buckled. I tried to find Mary's face, but I couldn't see her because tears had already blurred my vision. I rapidly blinked them away, hoping to hear her deny the accusation, but she just stood there, legs spread apart, head high, blood rolling from her busted lip, an angry but defiant woman.

"She killed Judge Hutchins and his brother," Reed said. "You can't turn her in. That's one thing your association made clear. If anyone caught the killers of Judge and his brother, they'd answer to us. Well, two of 'em have. Time we finish the job, Mister Hart."

Chapter Twenty

A mournful wind moaned through the valley as I stared, struck dumb at the sight of Judge's watch.

"You got something to say for yourself?" Captain Hart asked.

Mary had something to say, all right, but it's nothing I can repeat in polite company. I still picture the hurt in the captain's face at her response right before he pivoted, his spurs singing as he walked around his horse, fishing something out of his saddlebags that I couldn't see until his head tilted backward, and I caught the flash of pewter and knew the captain was finding courage, or escape, in his whiskey. Swallowing, he fastened his saddlebags, fidgeted with the saddle, and stepped back toward us. My mouth dropped open.

He carried his lariat.

"Like husband," one of the older hands said with a sneer, "like wife."

I should spend a moment describing Mary's camp. It lay on the valley's east side, partially hidden by piñon and juniper. The corral held only horses, with rotting hay piled up in a lean-to. In front of the corral sat a square, rock house that had lost its roof years earlier, though Mary and her pals had thrown a ripped tarp over the remaining *vigas* to provide some protection from the rain. A fine place for scorpions and rats, but not much else. The door to the house had also vanished, most likely chopped up for kindling, and three walls looked like they would collapse with a sneeze. The front wall remained sturdy, however, and the wooden beam above the doorway would serve as a handy gallows, piñons and junipers being too short for such a chore.

Ignoring Rex Steele when he held out his hand, the captain made a beeline for the rock house, tossing one end of the rope over the beam.

"You best say something, gal," Rex Steele pleaded.

Mary's eyes focused on the lariat as the captain backed away, his face haunting in its viciousness. Our other men remained just as quiet, looking at the hemp loop that would serve as a hangman's noose. Slim Reed was the only man who relished what was about to happen, the lone man capable of doing anything, it seemed. He walked to Mary, holding a rawhide string to secure her hands behind her back.

"Mary . . . ," Rex Steele's lips pleaded.

She spoke, trying to sound brave, but her voice cracked though her eyes matched the captain's in intensity. "You've been wanting to do this for twenty years," she said.

"If you had a hand in killing Judge and Fred, I'm done with you," Captain Hart answered.

"You've been done with me." She threw her head back and tried to laugh, but no sound came until she spoke again, softly yet bitterly. "Like you ever had anything to do with me."

When Slim Reed grabbed her arms, I shot forward, stumbling, crying out that she was innocent.

Reed stopped, but only because he dropped the rawhide.

"She couldn't have done it," I pleaded. "I saw her at the funeral. The funeral in Puerto de Luna. After the funeral, I mean. She was inside the church there, and, well . . . well, she told me that Judge was supposed to be or had been her godfather. Don't you see? She couldn't have done it. She wouldn't go to that church to pay respects, not if she had killed them!"

"Guilt." Slim Reed's voice chilled me as much as the hand he pressed on my shoulder. He spun me around. "She was feeling guilty, is all. Begging for His mercy. His mercy she can have, but not ours."

He shoved me past Mary, her hands still untied, toward my horse.

"You can't do this!" I yelled. "It ain't right!"

Nobody listened.

Nobody, except Kim Harrigan.

That old Brown-Merrill let out a deafening roar, sending about a half dozen horses to bucking, and he worked the bolt of the rifle, still sitting on his steady horse, and said: "Ain't nobody hangin' a woman again. Not even you, Capt'n."

"One against thirty, Harrigan?" the captain asked calmly.

I staggered to my horse, pulled out the shotgun, fighting with my awkwardness of being one-handed, and moved toward Mary and Slim, although no one paid me any attention. Every eye trained on Kim Harrigan, they didn't even see me.

"You wouldn't shoot us," someone said, and the next thing I heard was a shot.

The bullet knocked Kim Harrigan out of the saddle, and only then did I see Slim Reed. Using

Mary's body, he had shielded his move, palmed his pistol, and fired. Even I hadn't noticed him until his revolver barked, but, when he stepped from behind Mary, laughing, I pulled a trigger.

Now, what all happened next, I'm not rightly clear. Confusion, that's what it was. Hoofs pounding, my ears ringing, my broken arm aching instead of itching, and me lying on my backside, prickly-pear spines biting my thighs and the palm of my good hand. I couldn't see much, but I knew I no longer held the shotgun. A horse screamed, then another shot sounded, and I recognized it as Kim Harrigan's old cannon.

He's still alive! I thought.

Other voices, too, including one piteous moan followed by a roar of hatred. "I'll kill you, boy. God as my witness, you'll be deader than the Hutchins brothers or them two greasers!"

"First man that moves, I kill!" That sounded like Kim Harrigan.

"You can't shoot all of us, Harrigan." I didn't recognize that one.

"Nor can I, but I'll give one of you-all a belly full of buckshot!"

My eyes cleared, and there stood Mary Magdalene Holliday, holding the shotgun I had dropped, pointing the weapon in the general direction of the Hart riders. As I scrambled to my feet, I spotted Slim Reed lying in the mud, rolled up in a ball, and rocking, both hands gripping the bloody mess that had been his right calf. His shock-filled eyes locked on me, and I heard him repeat his threats. "You're dead, boy. Nobody does this to Slim Reed. . . ." Pain choked off his cries.

Beside his horse, Kim Harrigan knelt, his rifle

weaving, blood staining his left shoulder, spreading down to his waist. Somehow, he kept the Brown-Merrill pointed at Captain Hart, who stood next to the rock house, not moving, not even speaking, just glaring. He wasn't looking at Mary, not at Reed or his men, not even Kim Harrigan and the big rifle aimed at the captain's gut. No, Captain Hart stared long and hard—at me.

I looked away, had to, and darted to Old George, who held the reins to his horse in his left hand. "I'll take my pistol back, George," I said, trying to sound determined.

"Sure, Caleb." He removed the gun belt and passed it to me, even helped me buckle it on. That had to be a peculiar sight. Then I stepped away from him, drawing the little double-action gun. "You men step off your mounts and go pile your six-shooters in the rock house yonder. Go on. Anybody who breathes wrong, gets shot!"

No one moved.

"You-all better move!"

"Do as the kid says." It was Rex Steele who spoke, and, to my surprise, the men obeyed. I mean, there were thirty Hart riders against us. Mary had only one shell unfired in the shotgun, Kim was wounded, swaying on his knees with a bolt-action rifle, and I was just a fourteen-year-old greenhorn, my gun hand shaking violently. Maybe that's why they obeyed. They weren't gunmen, but cowboys. The one man-killer, excepting the captain, lay writhing on the ground, bleeding worse than Kim Harrigan, spitting out saliva and threats against me. Maybe they just followed Rex's orders, or didn't want to see Captain Hart get killed. Or perhaps the idea of hanging a woman didn't set well with them, either. I half expected one of them to dive behind the safety of the walls of the rock house, grab a gun, and cut us all down. Yet they surrendered, meekly, without a fight. The only person who didn't move was the captain.

His eyes never left me. The big Schofield .45 remained in his holster.

"Shuck it!" Mary barked at him.

He didn't even blink. She turned the shotgun from the cowhands to his stomach. Still, he remained a statue.

"Rex," Mary said, "if you don't want to have to pick up your boss' guts. . . ."

With a sigh, Rex Steele slowly drew the heavy revolver from the captain's holster and tossed it into the rock house. Then he unbuckled his own gun belt and pitched it inside.

"Now what?" Rex asked.

Which is what I was thinking? There had to be maybe 200 raiders raising dust all over southeastern New Mexico. Where would we go? Before we could even consider that matter, how did we plan on getting out of this spot?

"You boys start walking toward San Patricio," Mary ordered.

"And what of him?" Jesús Salazar asked in Spanish, pointing at Slim Reed.

"Carry him if you want, or leave him to rot," Mary answered.

Slowly the Hart riders turned and began walking away. Just like that. Old George wrapped a bandanna over Reed's calf, used another rag and a stick as a tourniquet, then he and Salazar carried the gunman, screaming with every step, toward the line of cowboys. The last man left was Captain Hart, and he kept those wolf eyes boring through me for the longest time.

"We'll hunt you down," he finally said, his words even, cold. "You got nowhere to go."

"Maybe I'll try Mexico," I said, all bluster. My mouth tasted of gall, and I thought I'd just collapse and throw up.

"No one crosses me," he said. "You chew that thought until you see me again, boy, because . . . brother's son or not. . . ."

Holstering the .32, I stood my ground.

"You once told me something, Captain," I said, lips trembling. "Right after Slim Reed killed Earl Sutton. You told me that we do what's right, said that's what Grandpa taught you and Papa. 'You always side with what's right.' That's what you said. Not what the law says is right, but what your gut tells you is right. Well, that's what I'm doing now. Now, you best start walking."

I think he gave me a nod. Maybe it's my imagination, wishful thinking, but that's how I picture things. I sure didn't imagine what he told me before he strode away.

"I'll be doing what I think's right, too."

Once they were maybe 100 rods away, we stopped dawdling. I mean, I stopped. Mary took charge, and there wasn't any question who led our group of rebels. She barked at me to help Kim onto his horse, then moved to the corral to saddle her dun, pitching the shotgun to the ground in favor of her Winchester. As soon as I had Kim in the saddle and his rifle in its scabbard, I found Mary, holding the reins to her horse, staring down at the two men Slim Reed had killed. I walked over to her, not knowing what else I needed to do.

Head bowed, she whispered their names, names I've now forgotten. Crossing herself, she turned without another word and swung onto the big dun.

"You coming?" she said, glaring.

I stuttered and ran to Penny, struggled to get mounted, my heart pounding. My boots had just slid into the stirrups when Mary cut loose with her rifle, screaming at the top of her lungs. Penny did a little side-step, snorted, and jumped, but nothing I couldn't handle, and, when I finally recovered, thirty-odd Hart horses were loping into the hills.

"With luck," Mary said, "they'll skedaddle all the way to the ranch."

"Where to?" Harrigan spoke, his face pale.

Mary grinned, but I knew it was only a façade. "Mexico?" she asked me.

"No," I said, surprised to be that sure of myself. "They'll expect that. Puerto de Luna. Puerto de Luna," I repeated with a nod. "And Grandma Anna."

"She ain't nothing to me." Mary's smile had gone.

So had my patience. "Nobody's nothing to you!" I said, adding an oath. "That's your problem. You blame everyone for all your misery. All I know is Grandma Anna told us to come to her if we're in trouble, and, by grab, we're in trouble. Besides, Puerto de Luna lies just north of the captain's range. We might could find help there."

She tilted her head toward Harrigan. "And him? You thought about your pal with the big gun? It'll take us five, six, seven days to ride to

Puerto de Luna. Maybe more, if he lives. And you don't even know the way."

"I do." My head swung toward Kim's weary voice. He didn't say anything else, but tugged the reins and turned his horse. I kicked Penny into a walk and followed. Muttering a curse underneath her breath, Mary came with us.

By the time we rode through Lincoln, the clouds had burned off, giving us a right pretty New Mexico day. It was Mary's decision to ride through Lincoln, but, when I saw all those folks looking at us, I questioned her judgment. *Stupid*, I thought. Men, women, and children watching us, like they must have done whenever Billy the Kid or any of that crowd would come visiting. We should have skirted around town. Now they could tell the captain they saw us, but, Mary explained, he might think we were trying to fool him. Besides, from Lincoln we could go anywhere, west, north, or south. Anywhere but east, and all that wide open Hart land.

Past the Wortley Hotel, we turned off the road for the Río Bonito, its waters deep and swift from all that rain, crossed it without a problem, and Mary kicked her dun into a trot and took the point. She led us to a forested cañon, and we began climbing toward the Capitans.

I didn't like this cañon at all. Seemed like a trap to me, and I liked the way Kim looked even less. He had plugged his bullet hole with a handkerchief, but that chunk of lead was still inside him. I don't know how he managed even to stay in his saddle. When I tried to ride up alongside him, to offer assistance, he barked at me: "Stay clear of these walls." His head tilted forward, and I spied an eight-foot rattlesnake sunning itself on the ledge. "Lined with rattlers," he said.

I obeyed, and kept my eyes trained on the walls, the hoofs of our mounts clopping noisily over the rocky trail. Mary didn't say much, but she knew this country. Once she led us to a water hole, and we stopped to let the horses drink.

"You want to rest?" she asked Kim. "Sit in the shade a spell?"

His head shook. "If I get down, I might not be able to get up."

"If you don't get down," I said, "you'll bleed to death in that saddle."

"Bleedin's stopped," he said. "I'll rest later. But I want you to do me a favor." He stared right at me. "Lash my hands to the saddle horn, Caleb, with my bandanna."

He didn't slide out of the saddle, however, until we made camp early that evening at the top of the Capitans. The clouds had returned, as they always did that spring, and the wind blew like a gale. We had hardly any grub, only our soogans to keep us warm, and Kim spent the whole night tossing feverishly while we rocked, shivered, froze. That was about as nasty a night as I ever spent on the trail, us running a cold camp, the gap serving as a funnel for a brutal wind that howled without cease.

When dawn finally came, the wind was still blowing hard. Awakened by low groans, I stiffly tossed off my soogans and found Mary kneeling over Kim. Slowly she turned to me and said: "That bullet had better come out."

Chapter Twenty-One

"Not hardly." Kim said through a tight grimace. When his head turned toward me, I grimaced. Beads of sweat dotted his forehead and bald pate, despite it remaining mighty cold that frosty morning, and he was deathly pale. "We need to get off this mountain." A coughing fit stopped him. "Put some. . . ." Another racking cough. "Distance between us . . . and Capt'n. . . ."

"At least he ain't bleeding," Mary told me while still tending to Kim. "I put a mud and moss poultice on it." She wiped the sweat off his face with a rag and gave him a weak smile. "But that lead in your shoulder will poison. . . ."

"Tomorrow," he said hoarsely. "Now help me up."

We rode easy that morning, following a game trail through thick pines, watering our horses at a bubbling creek that Mary said hadn't been flowing in years. She dropped from the dun, her feet swallowed by mud, soaked a bandanna in the flowing water, then passed the cloth to Kim, who wiped his face. The clouds had burned off by noon, and we cleared the forest and rode along a ridge. To the north below stretched the flat open spaces where we'd soon be traveling. I didn't like that, suddenly preferring mountains and forests for hiding places, but there was no other way to get to Puerto de Luna.

"Let's pick up the pace," Kim said, nudging his mount into a trot. Even with his wrists bound to the horn, I'll never know how he stuck to his saddle, with us crossing deep gullies, the wind and sun whipping our faces. I kept looking for vigilantes, but saw only cholla, much of it dead, and acres and acres of prickly pear. Recalling her fear of cactus, I kept a tight rein on Penny.

Nerves taut, we camped that night in the open to wake up to another bitterly cold morning thick with fog and mist. Mary had a fire going in a little rock shelter, boiling water and the last of our beef jerky in a tin cup. Her folding knife lay open, the blade on glowing coals. Kim sat near the fire, violently shivering. Soogans covered his legs, and draped over his shoulders were our three saddle blankets. Wet as they were, blankets and soogans were all we had to keep him warm. Mary picked up the cup, set it aside to cool, and turned the blade over.

"Bullet's coming out," she told me. "You'll have to hold him down, Caleb, when I go digging with this knife. You think you can do that for me, one-handed and all?"

I couldn't speak. Not even sure how I managed to nod.

"All right. Kim . . . Kim, can you hear me? Here. Take this. Watch it, it's hot. Closest thing to broth I could make, but ain't much more than hot water. Don't have no whiskey, either, and I'm sorry for that 'cause this is going to hurt something fierce. So drink. There. Good. All of it. Good man."

After vomiting it up almost immediately, Kim fell back. "Hold him!" Mary yelled, and I straddled his body, pressing my filthy cast against his wounded arm, pinning the other one in cold, wet grass with my good hand. Mary pulled open his shirt, tossed her bandage and poultice into the mud, and slid the hot blade into the ugly wound.

Kim's eyes shot open, wild with fright, and he let loose with a savage scream. I threw up myself from the stench, the sounds, the horror of it all, emptying my stomach onto the ground near Kim's side. Mary ignored me, wiping a mixture of nervous sweat and rain water from her own face before probing deeper with the blade. Thankfully Kim Harrigan passed out. I wanted to join him.

That afternoon, when the gloom had vanished again and God blessed us with, if only temporary, sunshine, Mary had me saddle up Penny and scout around. Kim lay sleeping, no longer tossing, either, and a little bit of color seemed to have returned to his face, but he was still in bad shape. Mary had dug out the flattened hunk of lead, then heated the blade again to cauterize the bullet hole. Don't reckon I'll ever forget that. Smell of that burned flesh stuck with me for years.

Let me tell you about Penny. To me, she was the hero. I had ridden about a mile, not seeing much, circling around slowly, not even knowing what I was really looking for. Penny's shoes clip-clopped as she walked up a little ridge, but the sound her hoofs made suddenly changed to a hollow thumping. I didn't know it at the time, but we were standing on what might soon turn into a sinkhole. You know this country; it's littered with sinkholes, some full of the deepest, bluest water you'll ever see. Well, once atop the ridge, I scanned the horizon, looking for vigilantes, but found only swaying grass and more cholla. Then out of the corner of my eye, I spotted something else.

It was a rattlesnake, and it crawled underneath Penny's belly, but, calm as she was, she just stood there. Had I been on Chuck, or another horse, I probably would have got dusted, but Penny acted as if she didn't even see the serpent, and maybe she hadn't. My first thought was to grab my lariat, dismount, and whip the snake to death the way I'd seen Kim do it. Yet I didn't trust my skills with a lariat, and certain-sure didn't want to get snake bit or left afoot.

It's a good thing, too, because I detected more movement, and here crawled another rattler, this one twice the size of the first one. Another one appeared, then another, and I understood that we had stopped right smack on top of a den of snakes. Still, Penny remained still. By jacks, I shook in my stirrups more than she moved. When the last of the rattlers had crawled away, I put the spurs to that mare's flanks, and we got off that hilltop in a hurry, I mean to tell you.

Yes, Penny was some horse, and she'd save my bacon again.

Somehow managing not to get lost, I returned to camp. Awake now, Kim claimed he was ready to ride, and, against our better judgment, we lit out, keeping the pace slow for Kim's sake, and our own.

Up and down those rocky, high, rolling swells we rode. The hills, covered with nothing but bear grass and cholla, became smaller as we journeyed

south. This country was vast—reckon I truly noticed it for the first time—the blue sky immense.
When we rested a bit around mid-afternoon in a
shady cañon underneath a raven's huge nest,
Mary again sent me on a scout.

Once again, I was glad to have had Penny with
me. Didn't see any rattlers, but, as I rounded the
corner of a rocky arroyo, I ran smack-dab into
two vigilantes, one mounted on a sorrel, the other
checking the left hind foot of his roan. They had
their pistols cocked, and I stared into two cav-
ernous muzzles before I knew what had happened.

"Who are you?" snarled the man on horseback,
a leathery, buck-toothed, heavy-set cuss.

They were scouting for Darius Rosecrans's
raiders, and didn't believe me when I told them I
rode for the Hart brand and that the captain had
sent me on a scout.

"Frank Hart don't send boys to do a man's
job!" the second man said.

"I am a Hart," I growled back. "Broke this arm
chasing rustlers. I'm as much of a man as you two
milksops."

Well, that wasn't the smartest thing to say, because the thinner man holstered his Remington,
walked over, and jerked me out of the saddle. The
breath exploded from my lungs when I landed on
my back, and pain sliced through my bum arm.
My head lifted just in time to feel the toe of a
boot. That's the last thing I remembered until a
horse snorted an hour later, and my eyes snapped
open to see Mary Magdalene Holliday dabbing
my bruised forehead with a wet rag.

"Come looking for you," she explained. "Thought you might have gotten lost." She sighed. "Looks like we both got snared."

I groaned. A moment later, the man with the bad teeth jerked me to my feet and shoved me forward. "Start walkin'," he barked, and pushed Mary after me. "You, too."

"Where are we going?" I asked.

"To get that third member of your party, boy. We'll let Mister Rosecrans decide whether to hang y'all or not."

Feeling Mary had betrayed Kim, I shot her my meanest glance. "We can't leave Kim alone. He'll die," she said. I knew she was right.

Now, here's where luck plays into things. Or maybe it was God's will. The thin man's roan had lost a shoe in the rocks, and, not wanting the gelding to go lame, he mounted Penny. The buck-toothed gent rode his own horse, pulling the roan and Mary's dun behind him.

A half hour later, spying the cañon wall and raven's nest, I wondered if I could somehow warn Kim. The man riding Penny read my mind and spurred up alongside me, leveling his Remington at my temple.

"One word, boy, and I splatter your brains over your lady friend's face."

He walked Penny alongside me, that big .44 just inches from my temple, and I knew then what I had to do. I kept walking, Penny right by me, picking our path, leading us right to a mound of prickly pear and cholla.

Boy-howdy, it wasn't much of a rodeo, but it sure served its purpose.

Cactus scared the daylights out of that mare, and she exploded like a bronc'y mustang, arching her back, leaping sky-high, and sending the thin man sailing. I didn't pay him any mind, just whipped around and charged the buck-toothed man. He saw what was happening, only couldn't react quick enough, tossing away the reins to Mary's dun and the roan, pawing for a long-barrel Colt. I reached to him before his pistol cleared the holster, clawed at him with my good hand, and, fighting his own skittish horse, he dropped the Colt as I pulled him from the saddle. Well, maybe the bucking sorrel had more to do with it than my pulling.

We crashed to the ground with a *thud*, and, when he lifted his head, I smashed it with my cast.

The pain in my arm sent me back on my hindquarters, but the buck-toothed man lay limp on the rocks. I don't think the hard plaster hurt him as much as the rock his head hit, but he was out of the fight. So was I. With the world spinning and my eyes filling with tears, I fell on my back, chest heaving, lungs burning. I hadn't forgotten about the thin man; I just didn't care any more.

"You all right?"

It was Mary's voice, and I looked up, wet my lips, tried to answer her.

"How . . . ?"

"Knocked cold. Both of them." She grinned. "I tied them up, run the sorrel horse off. Most likely, they'll free themselves in an hour or so, or Rose-crans'll come looking and find them, so we'd best light out of here. I'll fetch our horses and get Kim. You sit here, Caleb. You rest."

She helped me sit up, and, eyes closed, I waited for the dizziness and nausea to pass.

"That was a crazy thing to do," I heard her saying. "You could have got your head blowed off."

My head bobbed in agreement, but then changed directions, shaking now. "Had to," I said. "Had to protect . . ."—by some Herculean effort, my eyelids rolled open—"you."

She looked so lovingly then, not the hardscrabble twenty-year-old I had known, not the woman full of hate. She looked innocent, sweet, as if what I had said had penetrated her calloused heart.

"Caleb." I liked the way she said my name, and her hands reached out, her fingers gently running through my hair, and she pulled me close. Her lips felt so moist. It was my first kiss, not passionate—for Mary understood something about us that I hadn't quite grasped—but sweet, ginger. When I opened my eyes, Mary smiled.

I ran my fingers across my quivering lips, stared at this beautiful creature, and said: "You taste just like my grandmother."

With a snort, Mary spit out snuff, tossed back her head, and laughed long and hard. "You got a lot to learn," she said, still chuckling as she walked off to catch our horses and fetch Kim Harrigan.

Chapter Twenty-Two

By God's grace, we never ran into raiders as the days and nights wore on, just hundreds of sheep.

"Ought to stay clear of the ewes," Mary warned us. "They're lambing. And a mama sheep ain't like a cow. If she runs off, she'll never come back to her baby, and the coyotes'll get the lamb."

"Good," Kim said with contempt. "They're sheep."

I found Mary's reaction strange. A woman who rustled cattle, as hard a rock as you'll ever see, who didn't even flinch when facing a lynching, yet she'd ride out of her way to save a dumb lamb. Kim, now him I understood—sometimes. As a cowman, he hated sheep, but he was sure glad when we come upon a sheepherder who didn't speak English, the only person we'd seen since our little row with the Rosecrans riders.

Although his brow remained knotted with worry, the Mexican fed us mutton—the first solid food we'd had in ages—and gave us hot chicory to drink. The food did Kim a world of good, not that he'd ever admit it.

"You ride for *Señor* Hart?" the sheepherder asked in Spanish, after reading Penny's brand.

"*Sí*," I agreed, but I just couldn't lie to the old man. "We did. Now we ride from *el capitán*." My

Spanish wasn't that good, but the man nodded as if he understood.

"*Vaya con Dios*," he told us as we left.

Behind us, Capitan Gap had long faded from view, replaced by this wonderful country where the hills waved like an ocean. What hadn't changed was the weather. More clouds and more misting rain, which would leave as the days warmed only to settle back over us each evening and morn. All during this time, Mary stayed close to Kim, sending me out on morning and evening scouts. She changed his poultice—using ever-handy prickly pear, the spines burned off—and washed the wound with rain water she collected in a coffee cup each morning. Infection hadn't set in, and Mary finally conceded that Kim Harrigan might just live. They laughed at that, laughed a lot those days.

This country could surprise you, the way it changed. One day we were avoiding sheep, then suddenly dropped into cañon country, peppered with verdant cedar breaks, juniper, and oak brush. The trees were the first we'd seen in days, a sight to behold after nothing but cholla and bear grass. It reminded me of the land around Puerto de Luna, and I thought we were almost to Grandma Anna's.

"No," Mary said. "We got some traveling to do yet."

At camp that evening, I found true wonders of nature: "hexagons", six-sided stones shaped perfectly with beveled edges. I slipped a few in my pocket, and the next day I picked up another odd little stone. We were nooning on a rugged ledge

with Mary, for once, doing our scouting. I showed
my latest find to Kim.

"You becomin' a geologist?" he asked.

"No," I answered brusquely, and turned the
stone over in my hand. Somehow, nature had
shaped it into a perfect diamond shape.

"They call it a Pecos diamond," Kim said with
a tired grin. "Why don't you give one to Mary?
Ain't you sweet on her?"

My head shook. "No. She's my . . . cousin."

That's when it hit me. Mary Magdalene Holliday was kinfolk. Guess I had been starry-eyed
over her since we'd first met all those weeks ago
back in the Capitans, not knowing our bloodline,
yet when she had kissed me, it wasn't the great
lightning bolt I had expected, but a motherly kiss,
sweet, loving, but not romantic. Recalling our little exchange—"You taste just like my grandmother." . . . "You got a lot to learn."—I broke out
laughing, feeling a measure of relief, and of un-
derstanding, but the laugh died away when I saw
Kim's reaction.

"She's your . . . what?"

He didn't know. "Cousin. Rex told me. She's
the captain's daughter."

"Daughter! And he was set to hang her?" He
grimaced, shaking his head, rubbing the top of
his shoulder, before his eyes locked on me again.
The surprise, shock, anger left him, replaced by
some sort of curiosity.

"I knowed cousins to marry," he said.

I gave him a snort and spit worthy of Mary
Magdalene Holliday, and tossed the Pecos diamond to Kim, although I did gather up others for

any future sweethearts I might meet. (My wife has a couple in her jewelry box.)

What I didn't realize until that night was that Kim's last comment had been what you'd call fishing. Sorting out my intentions, you see. I might have been green, but I sure knew what was going on when Kim, that sly fox, placed the Pecos diamond in Mary's hand. Not long afterward, I excused myself to tend our mounts when she leaned forward and gave him a kiss, which didn't look so motherly. Unlike me, Kim Harrigan didn't mention that Mary tasted like snuff. Maybe because she had removed the dip and taken a swallow from her canteen before they embraced.

We had camped in a valley, peaceful, endless, surrounded by plateaus that reached 3,000 or 4,000 feet in elevation. Tomorrow we'd reach Fort Sumner. With luck, we'd been in Puerto de Luna the day after or the next.

"Luck's been with us so far," Mary said that night.

Luck was about to run out, though.

When Kim's shoulder started paining him an hour or so after we'd left Buffalo Springs the following day, we stopped to rest, and Mary sent me on another scout. I cut through gullies, anxious, worried, for we were near Fort Sumner now, and, while it might not be St. Louis, it was a busy crossroads where Hart and Rosecrans riders were known to buy whiskey.

The sheep were gone, but Hart beef scattered as I cautiously approached the Pecos, its banks thick

with brush, flies, and swarming mosquitoes. I
spied the road across the river, but saw no riders,
just more cattle, and beyond that a grove of cottonwoods shading a large adobe house. Still, no
people.

Clucking at Penny, I turned us around and
eased her into an easy lope. Best I could figure,
we could wait for dark in the gully where I'd left
Mary and Kim, skirt around town, head back
down to the Pecos, and enter the valley of Puerto
de Luna.

Leaning back in the saddle, I gave Penny
plenty of rein and let her pick her own path down
the steep embankment, then followed the winding path toward Mary and Kim. Nothing regis-
tered, not at first. Their horses stood grazing, and
Kim and Mary sat hunched against the far side of
the embankment, hands behind their backs.
Mary's head shook savagely, as if she were trying
to talk, yet no words came out. Stupidly I rode on,
scratching my itchy arm with a dead piece of this-
tle I'd picked up not long ago. Something was
wrong, but I couldn't figure it out. Suddenly, just a
few rods away, I knew. Mary couldn't talk because
somebody had gagged her with a bandanna. About
the time I reined in Penny and reached for my .32,
Mary freed herself of the cloth.

"Run, Caleb!" she shouted. "He means to kill
you!"

A blood bay mare and blue-clad rider exploded
out of nowhere, hidden behind a bend in the
arroyo, and I recognized his vile curse. I whirled,
spurring Penny, hunching forward, feeling the
mare pound the sides of the steep gully as we
climbed into the openness. I forgot the revolver in

my hand. A shot sang over my shoulder. I spurred harder, the wind whipping my face.

Newspapers said Slim Reed had killed more men than John Wesley Hardin, but I think the number is probably closer to twelve, a third of those coming after being hired by the association. Still, he came close to adding me to his total.

Urging Penny on, I snaked through the brush, heard two more shots from Reed's nickel-plated Colt. The gunman moved closer, Penny faltered, and we hit the Pecos River, splashing wildly. Someone screamed. Reckon it was me.

Then Penny was down, lying on her side, trying to lift her head out of the current, flakes of blood misting from her nostrils, bleeding hard from two holes in her side. Shot as she was, she ran her heart out, got me halfway into the river before she had nothing left to give. Hated to leave her like that, but, if I stayed, I'd be killed, for here came Reed. Crying, I plowed through thigh-deep water, reaching a sandbar in the river's center. I gripped the Harrison and Richardson, only never thought to use it. That's because fear gripped me, paralyzed everything but my legs.

Slim Reed's mare pulled alongside me.

"You're dead!" he shouted, yet the next thing I heard was him screaming, swearing, and the bay horse snorting, flailing, sinking, spraying me with mud. I tried to run faster, but couldn't. Couldn't even move. A gunshot left my right ear ringing, but I felt no muzzle blast, no pain. My head jerked in time to see the blood bay mare, up to its chest in the mud, falling to its side, and Slim Reed diving over the horse's side.

His lower right leg had been splinted, and he

had dropped his Colt when he left the saddle. That's all I truly saw of him. The horse rolled over, floundering, kicking, trying to find solid ground. I had my own problems. I had sunk to my waist—and was sinking farther.

Quicksand!

The blood bay kicked violently. Slim Reed swore. I tried to run, tried to climb, crawl, swim out of the sandy muck, but only sank farther into the bowels of the Pecos.

"Help!" I yelled, trying to be heard over Reed's curses and the shrieks of the struggling horse. The Harrison and Richardson slipped from my hand. The moving, liquid ground immediately consumed it.

"Help me! Please!"

The trap had pulled me to my shoulders, now. I spit out mud and water, tears blinding me. I never heard the splashing hoofs, but, at the sound of Mary's voice, I blinked away that gut-wrenching panic, spotted her sitting on the dun in the Pecos, looping a lariat in front of me.

"Grab on, Caleb! Grab on tight!"

My right hand grasped frantically at the loop, gripped it, had no time to try to get it over my shoulders. Immediately Mary kicked the horse, and I felt the rope biting palm, fingers, and wrist, pulling, but I refused to let go. Pain sliced through my broken arm, too, and then I was free of the mud and muck, being dragged through the river, choking out thanks to God when I found myself on the bank. Quicksand had claimed my boots and socks, but not my life.

"You all right?" Mary knelt beside me.

I couldn't answer, simply collapsed on the soft

grass. Mosquitoes dined on my face, neck, and hands. Exhausted, I didn't care, until I remembered Slim Reed.

My head jerked up, and I saw Mary staring at the river. I looked, too, finding Reed's blood bay. Only the mare's head remained above the surface, its eyes wild with fear. Then even that vanished. A few rods away lay Penny, no longer moving, the water red with blood and mud as it flowed downstream.

And Reed? He had been trapped on the wrong side of the kicking mare. We never really knew if his mare's hoofs had killed him before the quicksand pulled him under.

A thousand questions raced through my mind, questions that wouldn't be answered for hours. Mary had freed herself from Reed's bonds, untied Kim, loped after me. Surprising them in the gully, Reed had cuffed Kim good, stepped on his bad shoulder, and dug in with the toe of his boot after Reed had knocked the fight out of him. Kim couldn't ride fast, could barely ride at all, but he had told Mary to go find me, swearing he'd catch up.

Yet we had time scarcely to catch our breaths. Galloping horses sounded down the road, and Mary leaped into the dun's saddle, pulling me up behind her. Sharp pain sliced up and down my bad arm, but I gripped her waist tightly as she raked the dun with her spurs.

Behind us, gaining on us, came Captain Hart and better than a dozen men.

Chapter Twenty-Three

Three, four shots whizzed over our heads as Mary's lathered horse pounded the road. Bullets kicked up sand in front of us, and then one slammed into the dun's head. He crashed hard. We crashed hard. My arm hadn't hurt this badly the time I had broken it, yet I scrambled to my badly skinned bare feet, spitting out sand, blood, limping. On rode the vigilantes.

I heard music. My first thought? Angels singing.

Jesus, Savior of my soul,
Let me to thy bosom fly,
While the waves of trouble roll,
While the tempest still is high. . . .

Through the pain, I saw an adobe wall that seemed vaguely familiar. The angels sang louder.

Hide me, oh, my Savior hide,
Till the storm of life is past;
Safe into the haven guide;
Oh, receive my soul at last.

My fog lifted. "Mary!" I shouted. She was clawing at the dun, trying mightily to free the Winchester that was pinned between the dead horse and the hard road. "Forget that rifle!" I bellowed, jerking her to her feet with my good hand. Another bullet rang out, followed by a thunderous roar that had to be Captain Hart. I pushed Mary toward the wall. "Come on!" I yelled, limping toward the open gate.

Inside, better than a dozen men in black, women likewise dressed with dark veils or black ribbons, and two or three children, all circling an open grave, now stared at us. The red-bearded circuit rider dropped his Bible to his side, glaring at us intruders. Hearing the gunshots, they had only sung louder, gunshots not being that rare in Fort Sumner. Only when Mary and I burst in did their singing cease. Gravediggers rose from their seats underneath the cottonwoods. No one spoke.

I scanned their bodies. Not one handgun, not one rifle. Well, it dawned on me, who brings a firearm to a burial? I looked for another way out of this cemetery, but found only adobe walls, and I shuddered at a thought: *I've led us to our own graves.*

All this I observed in fewer seconds than it takes to tell. Suddenly a palomino stallion exploded through the gate, and I spun to see Captain Hart. Ignoring the funeral possession, he swung from his horse, and I shoved Mary.

"Run! He'll kill you." I charged the captain. "Leave her alone!" I screamed, limping toward him, hurting all over. His backhand staggered me. I tripped over one broken cross, pounded my head against a marble tombstone. When I rolled over, tried to shake out the cobwebs, I found myself staring up at a revolver. Dickie Fergusson held it.

"Don't . . . ," Dickie pleaded.

I could barely hear him, but Mary's scream

shocked me to action. I rolled over, hoping Dickie wouldn't pull the trigger, crawled a couple of rods, but the cemetery kept weaving. I reached out, gripped a wooden cross, pulled myself to my knees.

"This ain't right," I said hoarsely, but no one heard me.

Captain Hart towered over Mary, who, crawling herself, had backed up against the far wall. He stood over her, both of them shaking.

"You killed Judge Hutchins!" the captain bellowed. "And you must answer for it!"

"I didn't kill him!" Mary fired back.

Back in the valley south of Lincoln, she had never said a word one way or the other about those deaths. Truth is, we hadn't even mentioned it on our ride north, maybe because deep down I wondered if she had a hand in the slayings. Now, in the old post cemetery, I suspect all the graves unnerved her. Perhaps she realized that Kim Harrigan, wherever he was, and I couldn't save her. Maybe it was the captain's intensity. Whatever the reason, for the first time since I'd know her, Mary Holliday was frightened. Petrified.

"His watch!" the captain roared.

Her head shook. She was crying. "Ramón Chavez give it to me. In Puerto de Luna. To pay for those cattle I sold him. Your cattle!"

"You expect me to believe that?" He reached down, jerked her to her feet, shoved her toward the big cottonwood. The gravediggers scattered.

"Rex," Captain Hart barked, "let's get this hanging over with!"

I stood, but the world twisted rapidly, and I dropped to the sod again. My left forearm was ablaze in agony. The dizziness didn't seem it would ever pass. Inside my dry mouth I tasted blood. My feet burned. Rough hands, though trying to be gentle, helped me up. I saw Dickie Fergusson, his Colt holstered.

Stop it, I tried to say, but the words wouldn't come out.

"Let her be!" a frail voice resonated from the crowd of mourners. "She's telling the truth, Frank!"

I blinked. It couldn't be, but it was.

Grandma Anna stepped out in front. "I saw Chavez with that watch. Didn't know it was Judge's. That rapscallion of a butcher likely bought it from the men who really killed them. Turn her loose, Frank. Turn her loose, I say!"

For once in his life, the captain stood, wavering, uncertain. "You'd say anything . . . to protect. . . ."

"My grandchild?" Grandma Anna laughed. "Yes, I would, but it's the truth. Turn her loose. For God's sake, you're both Harts!"

The captain's head shook in defiance, or something else. "No, she killed Fred. She killed Judge. She. . . ."

"Fred and Judge don't have a thing to do with this, Son." My grandmother began walking toward them. "And you know it!"

His voice cracked. "She . . . killed . . . Consuela!"

"She died giving birth," Grandma Anna said. "Giving birth to your daughter, and you've blamed this child all these years for your wife's death. I always let my boys do as they see fit, but no more, Frank. No more. You're wrong, just as wrong as I've been for never saying so before now." Only feet from Captain Hart and Mary, she halted. Her finger pointed to me. "Like you killed the horse that broke Caleb's arm. You blamed the horse. But not really. It was you that you blamed. Like you blamed yourself for your brother's misery and hardships. Like you blamed yourself for letting this child marry that no-account, Thaddeus Holliday. Like you blamed yourself for Colby King's death. Like you blamed yourself for everything, even your father's passing, only you never could admit it, so you blamed others." Her voice rose with a savagery I'd never heard. "Well, you think Consuela would approve. You think your wife wants your daughter dead. Go ahead, Son. Hang her!"

Captain Hart turned, stumbled, looked back, first at Grandma Anna, then toward his men crowding the gate, next at me, finally at Mary. His knees buckled, and he fell, muttering her name, supporting himself by gripping a weathered marble monument. He reached for her, but she jerked from his touch, and then Captain Hart's head bowed, and he was crying, choking, sobbing without control, heart-broken.

Yet Mary did a peculiar thing. Her right hand lifted toward him, too, but only briefly, then dropped to her side. Her lips mouthed— "Daddy."—but she spun on her heels, moved away from him.

Grandma Anna, however, had also seen it, and she wrapped an old arm over her granddaughter's shoulder, leading her toward the gate. Her smile widened when she neared me.

"It's gonna be all right," she whispered to Mary, me, or herself—I don't know. "Everything's gonna be all right."

Captain Hart, he just rocked and cried. His hat

had fallen. He choked out words, but I understood few: "Lucas . . . Consuela . . . Papa . . . Mary. . . ."

"Get out of here!" Rex Steele suddenly barked. "All of you, get out of here."

"This is a funeral!" the circuit preacher snapped back.

"You don't do like I say," Rex said, "it'll be yours!"

They started walking.

"Come on, Mary," Grandma Anna said. Tears streamed down their cheeks. "We'll get you all cleaned up. I'd like to talk . . . well, let's . . . let's just see. . . ."

Hart riders parted, and Mary and my grandmother went through the gate and turned toward town.

Was it luck that Grandma Anna had been in Fort Sumner? God's will? Irony? She was there for a funeral, to bury the rustler my uncle's men had killed at Los Portales. Grandma Anna had known the man's mother, had come here out of respect, but she'd later tell me that something, someone had told her in a dream to be there that day.

Maybe she was there for her son. Since our set-to near Lincoln, almost a week earlier, the newspapers had turned on Franklin J. Hart. Captain Hart's Vengeance Raid no longer was spoken with reverence. Lawmakers and laymen, sheepherders and hog-farmers, merchants and marshals, women and even cowboys had had enough of killing. The hiring of Slim Reed would be a black mark haunting the Southeastern New Mexico Stock Growers' Association for years. New Mexico Territory had turned on Captain Franklin J. Hart. So had his world.

"You, too!" Rex Steele barked again, but now he was speaking to his own men. "Get out of here. Go on. Go on to the saloon. I'll join you directly! I said get . . . get out of my sight. Get, or I'll kill you!"

As the men filed through the gate, I spotted Kim Harrigan, who had arrived moments earlier. He leaned against the wall, holding the Brown-Merrill, but, so weak, the barrel was dragging in the dirt. His shoulder had started bleeding again, and I stumbled to him. He didn't see me at first, his eyes focused on the captain.

"I'm sorry!" I heard my uncle blubber. "God help me. . . ." Then more uncontrolled sobs, gasps, moans.

I wanted to cry myself, for Penny left dead in the Pecos, for Mary and Kim and Grandma Anna, and all the emotions boiling up inside me, but mostly for Captain Hart. "You're both Harts," my grandmother had said. Well, I was one, too.

"Get out of here, Caleb," Rex Steele said, but without any threat in his voice.

The rifle slipped from Kim Harrigan's fingers, fell in the dirt, and I put my good arm around his back. He stared at my bare feet. "What happened . . . ?"

I let out a weary sigh. "I'll tell you later. Come on. Best get you to a doctor."

"You could use one, too, Caleb," Rex said. "You seen Slim Reed?"

My head had cleared, though my arm still hurt. I spit out blood from my busted lip. "No one will ever see him again."

"Get out of here," Rex repeated, still softly, without malice. "There's a sawbones in town. Not much of one, but . . . go on. Go on. I'll . . . I'll take care of Frank."

Yet Rex didn't move. As Kim Harrigan and I helped each other away, soon assisted by Salazar and Dickie, the Hart foreman bowed his head, not far from where Billy the Kid lay buried beside two of his companions. **PALS,** read that tombstone.

Which reminded me of Rex Steele and Franklin J. Hart. It also brought to mind a grave up on the hill at the Hart Ranch. The grave of Frank Hart's wife, dead these twenty years. Hallowed ground, Hobbs Wallace had called it. Hallowed it was.

The captain had fallen now, his back against the cottonwood's base, alone. We limped out of the cemetery, leaving Rex Steele with the captain, moving toward the rawhide little town, nobody speaking, the wind moaning, but the sky clear, blue, with no threat of rain. Above the wind, I could still hear my uncle's sobs. Eventually Rex would walk away, too, without a word, leaving Captain Hart with the graves, the wind, and his own ghosts.

Epilogue

So here we are, gathered on this wind-swept hill, paying our last respects to Franklin J. Hart, burying him, as we know he would have wanted, beside his long-dead wife, Consuela. Burying him on one of the last remaining sections of Hart range. What once covered much of New Mexico has been reduced to a dozen square miles—the bulk of that state lease—a lot of country for most people, but scarcely enough for a rancher to make a living out here.

You've asked me to recollect my memories of Captain Hart, and I've told the story as best as I can, as true as I can. I'm right proud to see Mary here, glad that she and the captain settled things between them. Don't get any misconceptions. Reconciliation didn't come overnight. No, it took years, I reckon, but blood runs thick, especially Hart blood. The way I figure things, after calling a truce, they began to see each other for what they were, and why things had happened. The captain had hanged Mary's husband, but from what I've heard about Thaddeus Holliday, he probably saved Mary's life in doing so, and that might have been as much a reason for Holliday's lynching as was the killing of Colby King. Besides, months later, I recall Grandma Anna telling me that even if the captain had gotten a rope around Mary's neck, he wouldn't have hanged her. "How can you be so certain?" I remember asking, and she had smiled. "A mother knows her son."

Mary . . . well, she was the captain's daughter, the captain was her father, and they finally opened their hard-rock hearts. It's like Grandma Anna told them that day in Fort Sumner: "You're both Harts!" Point is, with time, lots of time, lots of anguish, they made things right, or as right as they could ever be.

Anyway, most of you-all know that it's Mary who has been running this ranch the past few years, since Captain Hart got too stove up, too sick, too old to work cattle, criminy, even sheep and goats. She has done it with his blessing, too, and done a mighty fine job.

Grandma Anna, she passed away a few years after I left New Mexico, died peacefully, with Mary and the captain at her side. 'Course, we all know what happened over in Hillsboro in '99, when those two gun hands, Oliver Lee and Jim Gilliland, were finally tried for killing Colonel Fountain and little Henry. It sickens me how they're both free, acquitted, though I guess I've never been quite sure if Lee was involved or not, but I'd bet my bottom dollar Jim Gilliland should have hanged. Still, I reckon the jury had problems since nobody has ever found the bodies, God rest their souls. Yet the law did right by the Hutchins brothers. Cannon Defroy and Tim Sutton, the scoundrels who really killed Fred and Judge and rustled their stock, were caught, tried, and hanged, legally, in '97.

I've lost track of most of the Hart riders from

those thirty-some years ago. Rex Steele, well, he's probably swapping lies and horses somewhere along the Pecos, but I'm happy to see—and I know Mary feels the same—Dickie Fergusson still mounted on Hart horses. Others, Hobbs Wallace, Jesús Salazar, Old George . . . they have all disappeared from my life. Even Kim Harrigan. Two years after the story I've just related, he up and joined the volunteers in Las Vegas, went to Cuba to fight the Spaniards, and never came back. Now, about all I have are the memories, but plenty of those.

As for me, I'm running a few head of cattle over in Arizona, in the shadow of the White Mountains, raising poled Herefords and a couple of kids. My brand is the Rafter H, but I guess, in many ways, I'll always be riding for the Hart.

Many say Frank Hart was a bad man, but we found good in him, too. What I know about cattle, about ranching and cow-boying, about people and love, right and wrong, a lot of that I learned during my stay here. I learned much about myself, too. I'm forty-seven years old now, the same age as the captain was back in '96, and, if I could tell Franklin J. Hart one thing, it would be this, something I reckon he would understand and appreciate.

I'm the man I am today, because, in the spring of my fourteenth year, I rode for the Hart brand.

Caleb Hart
May 5, 1929
South Camp, Hart Ranch,
Lincoln County, New Mexico

AUTHOR'S NOTE

Although the Hart Ranch is fictitious, as are most characters in this novel, the disappearance of Colonel Albert Jennings Fountain and his son is based on actual events. Oliver Lee and James Gilliland (sometimes spelled Gililland) were tried in Hillsboro in a media sensation—New Mexico's trial of the century—in May and June of 1899, more than three years after the murders. After more than two weeks of testimony, the jury deliberated for seven minutes to reach a verdict of not guilty. Lee later served two terms in the state senate in the 1920s. The remains of the Fountains have never been found.

I owe thanks to Fred Grove (for the train story, which I let Kim Harrigan tell Mrs. Hudspeth); saddlemaker Will Ghormley; Kyla Thompson; the St. Louis Public Library; University of Texas at El Paso Library Special Collections; El Paso Public Library; Branigan Library of Las Cruces, New Mexico; New Mexico State Library; Vista Grande Public Library; Las Cruces Convention and Visitors Bureau; Fort Sumner State Monument; New Mexico State University's Rural Economic Development Through Tourism program; and the following books: *The Life and Death of Colonel Albert Jennings Fountain* by A.M. Gibson; *Pat*

Garrett: The Story of a Western Lawman by Leon C. Metz; *A Texas Cowboy* by Charles A. Siringo; *Tularosa: Last of the Frontier West* by C.L. Sonnichsen; and *Life on the Prairies: Settling the Llano Estacado* by Thelma A. Webber.

For the most part, the trail taken by Caleb Hart, Mary Holliday, and Kim Harrigan is one I traveled on horseback one long, grueling week as part of the "Last Ride of Billy the Kid" trail (endurance) ride from Lincoln to Fort Sumner in late April and early May 2005. I owe many thanks to the organizers of that ride for letting me tag along as a journalist, and would like to express my deep appreciation to the land owners for allowing us cross their range: Wally and Robbie Roberts of Hobbs, the Chessers of Burnt Well Guest Ranch near Roswell, and the Buchman family of Fort Sumner taught (and tolerated) me a lot.

An extra nod goes to our wrangler on that ride, young Dickie McIntosh, a true modern-day cowboy and lover of Western stories. I hope he enjoys this one. Plus, B. Rex Buchman keeps trying to teach me about horses. Thanks again, Dickie, for bringing my horse back after it stumbled at a lope and pitched me over its side. Unlike Caleb Hart, I came away only with award-winning bruises. And thanks, Rex, for not laughing, too hard, after that wreck.

Johnny D. Boggs
Santa Fé, New Mexico

ABOUT THE AUTHOR

JOHNNY D. BOGGS has worked cattle, shot rapids in a canoe, hiked across mountains and deserts, traipsed around ghost towns, and spent hours poring over microfilm in library archives—all in the name of finding a good story. He's also one of the few Western writers to have won two Spur Awards from Western Writers of America (for his novel, *Camp Ford*, in 2006, and his short story, "A Piano at Dead Man's Crossing," in 2002) and the Western Heritage Wrangler Award from the National Cowboy and Western Heritage Museum (for his novel, *Spark on the Prairie: The Trial of the Kiowa Chiefs*, in 2004). A native of South Carolina, Boggs spent almost fifteen years in Texas as a journalist at the *Dallas Times Herald* and *Fort Worth Star-Telegram* before moving to New Mexico in 1998 to concentrate full time on his novels. Author of twenty-seven published short stories, he has also written for more than fifty newspapers and magazines, and is a frequent contributor to *Boys' Life*, *New Mexico Magazine*, *Persimmon Hill*, and *True West*. His Western novels cover a wide range. *The Lonesome Chisholm Trail* is an authentic cattle-drive story, while *Lonely Trumpet* is an historical novel about the first black graduate of West Point. *The Despoilers* and *Ghost Legion* are set in the Carolina backcountry during the Revolutionary War. *The Big Fifty* chronicles the slaughter of buffalo on the southern plains in the 1870s, while *East of the Border* is a comedy about the theatrical offerings of Buffalo Bill Cody, Wild Bill Hickok, and Texas Jack Omohundro, and *Camp Ford* tells about a Civil War baseball game between Union prisoners of war and Confederate guards. "Boggs's narrative voice captures the old-fashioned style of the past," *Publishers Weekly* said, and *Booklist* called him "among the best Western writers at work today." Boggs lives with his wife Lisa and son Jack in Santa Fe. His website is www.johnnydboggs.com.

MAX BRAND®

Luck

Pierre Ryder is not your average Jesuit missionary. He's able to ride the meanest horse, run for miles without tiring, and put a bullet in just about any target. But now he's on a mission of vengeance to find the man who killed his father. The journey will test his endurance to its utmost—and so will the extraordinary woman he meets along the way. Jacqueline "Jack" Boone has all the curves of a lady but can shoot better than most men. In the epic tradition of *Riders of the Purple Sage*, their story is one for the ages.

ISBN 13: 978-0-8439-5875-1

ANDREW J. FENADY

Owen Wister Award-Winning Author of *Big Ike*

No mission is too dangerous as long as the cause—
and the money—are right. Four soldiers of fortune,
along with a beautiful woman, have crossed the
Mexican border to dig up five million dollars in
buried gold. But between the Trespassers and their
treasure lie a merciless comanchero guerilla band,
a tribe of hostile Yaqui Indians and Benito Juarez's
army. It's a journey no one with any sense would
hope to survive, or would even dare to try, except...

The Trespassers

Andrew J. Fenady is a Spur Award finalist and re-
cipient of the prestigious Owen Wister Award for
his lifelong contribution to Western literature, and
the Golden Boot Award, in recognition of his contri-
butions to the Western genre. He has written eleven
novels and numerous screenplays, including the
classic John Wayne film *Chisum*.

AVAILABLE MAY 2008!

ISBN 13: 978-0-8439-6024-2

"When you think of the West, you think of Zane Grey." —*American Cowboy*

ZANE GREY

THE RESTORED, FULL-LENGTH NOVEL,
IN PAPERBACK FOR THE FIRST TIME!

The Great Trek

Sterl Hazelton is no stranger to trouble. But the shooting that made him an outlaw was one he didn't do. Though it was his cousin who pulled the trigger, Sterl took the blame, and now he has to leave the country if he wants to stay healthy. Sterl and his loyal friend, Red Krehl, set out for the greatest adventure of their lives, signing on for a cattle drive across the vast northern desert of Australia to the gold fields of the Kimberley Mountains. But it seems no matter where Sterl goes, trouble is bound to follow!

"Grey stands alone in a class untouched by others." —*Tombstone Epitaph*

AVAILABLE JUNE 2008!

ISBN 13: 978-0-8439-6062-4